CONFESSIONS

OF AN

courtney cole

Lakehouse Press, 2012

This book is an original publication of Lakehouse Press.
All rights reserved.

Library of Congress Cataloging-in-Publication Data

Cole, Courtney.
Confessions of an Alli Cat/Courtney Cole --- Lakehouse Press trade
pbk.ed.
ISBN: 978-0615722214

Printed in the United States of America

Dedication

To Teri.
The world is definitely more fun with you in it. Thank you
for the toilet paper wars, the peeking over bathroom stalls
and the many, many things I can't mention here.
Thank you for being my friend.

Prologue

(Because you need a little explanation before you dive into insanity)

There are times in life when a person (who may or may not be me) finds out that the man she has been married to for the last fifteen years has been cheating on her.

During such a grievous event, this person (who, again, may or may not be me) might decide to throw sanity to the wind and ride the Crazy Train into Crazy Town.

While said woman is there, she might enjoy the scenery so much that she takes up residence. And after a while, she might grow to love her surroundings so much that she joins a Crazy Convent and lives there forever and ever and ever.

I should clarify though.

When I say she goes crazy, I'm not talking the kind of crazy where she needs a straight-jacket. I mean that she's harmless crazy. As in, she dates-a-younger-gigolo-and-uses-a-vibrator-for-the-first-time. It's the kind of crazy where she goes out and buys $10,000 dollars worth of shoes and gets Botox. And possibly gets laser surgery on her abs that she will never admit to in a million years. It's the kind of crazy where she probably needs her credit card taken away and shredded.

But that's the good kind of crazy, right?

Because everyone knows that there are good and bad kinds of crazy, just like there are good and bad kinds of fat. Her kind of crazy is like the avocado kind of crazy— the good kind. The kind a person's body needs to stay healthy and strong.

These things may or may not have happened.

Okay, they did.

And it may or may not have been me.

Okay, it was me.

And every bit is true and then some.

Except the part about the convent.

I went crazy for a while, not freaking insane. I'm a healthy red-blooded female in the sexual prime of my life. I need sex. I would rather get shot in the leg and have a Brazilian wax every hour on the hour than live somewhere where there are no men. Seriously.

But I digress.

Hi. My name is Alli. My husband of fifteen years cheated on me with every female in a twenty mile vicinity who was willing and had a heartbeat. I thought about going all Lorena Bobbitt on him and chopping his dick off. But I didn't.

Instead, I took him to the cleaners in our divorce and then I went crazy.

But it was the good kind of crazy.

And there's one thing about the good kind of crazy... it makes for a really good story.

This is my story.

Welcome to Crazy Town. I hope you enjoy your stay.

Chapter One

(Or: Why God invented BFF's)

"Allison, I'm telling you, you need to try this. Honest to God, it's been the best decision I've ever made for my hormones."

"Which is exactly why I shouldn't even consider it. I'm too old to be listening to my hormones."

Sara stops in the middle of the frozen food section of our very local grocery store and puts her hands on her hips, glaring at me with her big brown eyes.

"And if you don't take care of your hormones, who will? Rick the Dick?"

"Shhh, Sara!" I look around to make sure no one is listening to our conversation. I'm glad to see that, for the moment, we are alone.

"Well? Is he?"

"You know he's not."

"And we know *why* he's not, too. Because his dick has been in service to at least four other women that we know of. At this point, I'd be afraid it might fall off inside you if you went back for some."

"Oh my god, Sara, hush! Someone's gonna hear you!"

I look around frantically, but thank God no one has appeared around us. Sara stares at me, half imperiously and half with pity.

"I don't care and you shouldn't either! I'm tired of women acting like having sexual needs is a bad thing. I'm all about embracing it. Girl, I wasted twenty years of my life thinking vibrators were evil. I still can't figure out why the hell I listened to my mother."

I'm the one who stares imperiously now.

"Sara, a vibrator and a young hot guy are two totally different kinds of toys. If you were trying to talk me into getting a vibrator, I'd be all for it. But this is totally out of the question."

I watch Sara's ruby stained lips fall open.

"Holy shit, you don't have a vibrator? Allison, what the hell? Aren't you afraid that thing is gonna get cobwebs and shrivel up from lack of use?"

I feel myself blush when I look up and see a little old lady sitting in a motorized cart frowning at us. Holy shit. How did I miss her purple hair when I looked around a minute ago?

Please God, let her have forgotten her hearing aid today!

"All right. That's it," Sara says suddenly, reaching for the few items in my buggy and dumping them onto a shelf in one big heap. "We are going to the naughty store. Today starts the liberation of Allison. Or at least your hoo-hah. I'm making it my mission in life to help you let your inner cougar out of the cage. That bitch has been in captivity for far too long."

She takes my hand and whirls me around, abandoning my cart and dragging me toward the exit. Our heels click loudly on the scuffed floor, attracting the attention of everyone in our direct vicinity.

And so, of course, this is when Sara chooses to be even more obscene.

"I'm gonna find you the biggest plastic cock on the market and you're gonna use it if I have to tie you down and do it for you."

I want to effing die.

I am horrified to see the head of every bag boy turn in our direction, even more so when I recognize two of them. They go to school with Sophie, my 15-year old daughter.

"Ohmigod, ohmigod, ohmigod! Sara, shut up!" I hiss at her.

"I will if you'll move your ass. This needs to be fixed. Today. And there's no time like the present. Sophie won't be home for another two hours. That's just long enough for me to change your mind."

"Like that's gonna happen," I murmur. "Don't hold your breath, Sara."

"We'll see, Miss Sexually Repressed. We'll see."

****

One humiliating hour later, Sara and I are pressed together in front of my computer, flipping through an online catalog of men. Well, I say "men" lightly. These males are somewhere between guydom and manhood, with guydom being that place in which the masculine form of our species gets stuck for the several years after high school and surrounding college.

I can't believe I'm doing this.

"It just feels wrong to be looking at these kids in any kind of sexual way." I look uncertainly at my insane friend. She stares back unapologetically.

"Trust me, Allison. They *want* you to look at them that way. And they're not *kids.* They're legal."

I scroll past one that doesn't look a day over sixteen. "Cheese and crackers, Sara! This is *somebody's* kid! I guarantee you his mother doesn't know he's a gigolo."

"Cheese and crackers? Really?" She looks at me skeptically. "Besides, he's not a gigolo, you prude! He's an escort. Big difference."

"An escort who, at the end of the night for a little more cash, will have sex with people. What do you call that?"

Sara's laugh has a wicked edge to it. "I call it my good fortune."

"Sara, I'm serious."

"So am I. But look, this is how I see it. I'm helping Chaz live out his dreams, too. He's getting to do things and experience things that most men twice his age will never know."

"I'm sure that's true, but you're never going to convince me that a twenty-year old would normally have any interest in someone our age. For God's sake, Sara, I got out of the shower this morning and scared the shit out of myself when I passed the mirror. I actually wondered for a second whose body it was. I've got bags and bulges in places that should never be lumpy and there's some weird excess skin on the backs of my arms that makes me look like a flying squirrel. A flying freaking squirrel! What twenty-year old in his right mind would wanna have sex with a flying squirrel?"

"Damn it, Allison, would you stop being so down on yourself? Men don't see us that way. Thank God! They see these warm, soft, beautiful, sensual creatures that smell fantastic and fuck like wild cats. We know what we want and how we want it. They don't care that our arms look like Dumbo's ears. They care that we can suck a golf ball through a garden hose and make them come in two point two seconds flat."

"Sara!" My ears turn red.

"And you need to stop doing that, too. Loosen up a little. You know, it's not the end of the world to drop an F bomb or talk openly about a blow job. Don't you remember high school at all?"

"Of course I do. I remember falling in love with the guy I thought was my soul mate, getting pregnant with our beautiful daughter and having what I thought was exclusive sex with him for fifteen more years before finding out he was cheating on me."

"Damn, how long were you in high school?"

I sigh in exasperation. "Sara, I want to move on, but I need to do it slowly."

"That's exactly what you *don't* need, Allison. You need to reach down deep and find that wild, courageous girl you used to be before Rick the Dick put an arrow through your heart. And your vagina. You need to find the *real* you. The one he doesn't control anymore. And I'm here to help you. You like penis! No, you fucking love penis. You just need to remind your vagina of that. Girl, you've got this. You're totally going to own it."

I say nothing. Instead, I just stare at my best friend in the world. I know she has my best interests at heart. And I know she's the one person on the planet I can trust completely and utterly. So why am I balking? What do I have to lose? My life as I knew it before is over anyway.

"Fine. I'll give it one shot, but I'm not promising that I'll sleep with some random kid that's only a few years older than my child."

Sara squeals and throws her arms around my neck.

"Oh my god, we're gonna have so much fun!" She claps her hands excitedly before settling back down in her chair beside me. She slides the mouse over to me. "All right. Let's get your account set up while I'm here. You have to be sponsored by a member to even have access to the site. Then we'll find you a toy."

"I think I've seen enough toys for today," I say somewhat somberly.

"This is not a bad thing, Allison. It's a good thing." She stares at me for a few seconds then lays her hand on my arm. "Okay, let's do this. Pick the guy you like and I'll do the rest. Deal?"

"You sound like a creepy used car salesman right now," I announce. She glares at me with her Realtor of the Year for the Greater Las Vegas Area stare.

"I guess," I say with a sigh.

She grins triumphantly.

"Not the enthusiasm I was hoping for, but I'll take it."

****

"Mom, I really need this. Won't you at least consider it?"

Spatula in hand, I turn to look at my daughter. "Sophie, do you have any idea how much a private swim instructor probably costs?"

"No, but I'll get Dad to pay half and it won't be that bad. Mom, all the swimmers that are Olympic hopefuls have their own private coach. You know I'll never make it anywhere with Mr. Sullivan."

"Mr. Sullivan does a perfectly fine job, Soph. It's because of him that you won State last year."

"I know, Mom. But that's not good enough if I ever hope to make it to the Olympics. Please. At least say you'll consider it. Kayla even knows a guy who was on her college swim team. She says he'll do it until I can get good enough to qualify for another one. That probably means he'll be cheaper, too."

"Sophie—"

"Don't 'Sophie' me, Mom. You treat me like I'm some airheaded kid. I'm more responsible, more dedicated than any of the girls my age. I never get in trouble and my grades are almost perfect. Do this one thing for me. Pleeeeeease."

I look into the wide, pleading hazel eyes that are so like my own. This child is my one true weakness, my very own brand of Kryptonite.

"Fine. Get me some information on the guy Kayla knows. We'll start from there. But *you* are asking your father, young lady!"

Her smile is like a thousand watt bulb; beautiful, young and innocent. So like mine twenty years ago, back before Rick the Dick made me resent anything with a penis.

"I will. Thank you so much, Mom." She leans across the island and pecks my cheek.

She really is a good kid. I just have to ignore the parts of her that seem like Rick sometimes, like the crease she gets in her mouth when she glares at me. Or the way she stands when she is annoyed, with her hand on her hip and the glazed, pissed off look in her eyes. Her eyes are mine, but that particular look is Rick through and through.

I sigh. She's half Rick, but she's half me, too. And that makes her awesome. She's a good kid. And she's mine. Rick can go to fucking hell.

I sigh proudly. Sara would be proud of me. I might not have said the F word, but I definitely thought it without flinching.

That's fucking progress.

I grin.

****

I'm unpacking my briefcase from work the next day, looking for a file, when I come across the plastic bag holding the enormous dildo Sara bought for me.

Holy freaking hell.

I feel my cheeks get hot just thinking about it, much less looking at it.

I pull it out and set it to the side, far away from me. I continue digging around for the file but I find myself glancing again and again at the package. Then a sexy grin flits through my head.

Shade. What the hell kind of gigolo name is Shade?

Even as the thought runs through my head, I'm thinking it's a damn good one. It's a dark and sexy name for a dark and sexy guy. I had practically licked the computer screen when I saw him smiling at me. He's the sexiest thing I've ever seen. Even if he is close to half my age.

You're not forty yet, Allison, I remind myself.

At thirty-five, though, some days I feel like I might as well be. And it's for just that reason I'm considering Sara's proposition. I don't want this to be the sum total of my life. A single mother, divorcee and marketing executive with nothing left but my job and bitterness. I don't want the fun part to be over. That would be like admitting defeat, like letting Rick steal all the best years of my life. And I refuse to let that happen.

Surely the best is yet to come. Surely.

Spontaneously, I push everything off the bed. I try not to cringe at the mess of papers I'll have to clean up later and focus on tearing open the box containing the vibrator instead.

It looks like a ten inch totem pole and my fingers are shaking. I'm such a chicken shit.

I grit my teeth and return my attention to the penis in my hand. It has carvings along its pink-colored length, with a squirrel and a beaver on either side of the base. But they aren't carved. They're like tiny animals protruding from the bottom.

All of Bambi's friends, I think obtusely.

I can only imagine that the beaver goes in the front to stimulate one side while the squirrel's tail goes in…the back.

In the freaking back??

Even in the privacy of my bedroom, I blush.

Holy hell, Sara! What are you trying to do to me? A freaking squirrel tail? Could this be considered beastiality in any way, shape or form? Oh my god.

I dig out five AAA batteries from the bottom of the bag and insert them into the vibrator then switch it on. I giggle when the head of the plastic penis starts to rotate in a tight circle, and the beaver and squirrel start to pulsate.

Good lord.

Shaking my head at my friend's sex toy of choice, I turn it off and take it to the bathroom to wash it.

I let the water warm up and lather my hands with antibacterial soap before I grab it. I run my fingers along the soft yet firm plastic and let my mind wander. I find myself thinking about Shade again, which is exactly what my friend, the freaking devil herself, had in mind.

What is a guy who does gigolo-ry in his spare time hung like?

I remind myself that I have no intention of finding out. I'm just curious.

Really curious.

Would he be smaller than the vibrator? The same size? *Bigger??*

Just the thought of that makes a little gush of warmth rocket through me, which really surprises me. I thought I'd lost this particular type of adrenaline long ago. Suddenly, I'm very excited by my new toy and the image of my soon-to-be escort. I've got visions of his sugar plums dancing through my head.

Oh god, you're so twisted! That's a Christmas reference!

But maybe something new, something naughty and forbidden, is just what I need to shake nearly two decades with a traitor. Fifteen wasted Christmases with a pathetic, lying husband. It's time for a new and shiny Christmas, so maybe it's just what the doctor (or Santa) ordered. The doctor, in this case, being Sara of course.

I rinse the new vibrator in hot water, deciding to name it Geronimo since I'm jumping into all sorts of new things. As it warms in my hands, I picture the super-hot Shade again. I think of having my own personal boy-toy, a sex slave with no other goal than to please me, to make all my fantasies come true.

To my complete surprise, within seconds of this wanton fantasy, my panties are damp. Holy crap. But this shouldn't surprise me. I've spent almost two decades with someone who came in two minutes flat and then rolled over snoring within the next two minutes following. Obviously the thought of someone who is paid to dote on every sexual desire that I might have is...stimulating. Impulsively, I strip my panties off and walk half naked to the bed. In broad daylight.

I'm nervous.

Very nervous.

What if I get it stuck and Sophie comes home and finds me with a buzzing vibrator lodged in my vag and then she has to drive me to the hospital where I have to have it surgically removed?? And of course the scalpel would damage the nerves down there and I'd never be able to climax ever again.

I'm an idiot.

I know this.

I'm a sexually repressed idiot.

With a deep breath, I lie down on my back with my knees bent and I close my eyes again, picturing Shade. I flip the switch on the vibrator.

The beaver's nose trembles against my leg and I laugh at the thought that a beaver is going to stimulate *my beaver*. Ha. I spin Geronimo until he is positioned right where he should be. It feels like ants crawling on me for just a second and I grit my teeth. But the very next second, I have gotten used to the feeling.

And holy-fucking-pygmy-goats!

I have to suck in a breath to keep from gasping.

Sweet Mary Mother of God. A million shards of light are exploding in my crotch. All I need now is a Baptist choir to sing Hallelujah and jump around waving their hands in the air.

I suck in another breath and dare to move it a teench.

Dear God, if only it was Shade's tongue!

I'm a dirty, dirty woman.

I'm fantasizing about a boy whose tongue is surely only in college. And the rest of him, too, of course. But I can't help it. As Geronimo pushes me closer and closer to a precipice that I haven't even approached in years (make that EVER), the fantasy hits me head-on and I don't let shame stop me from having it.

I imagine that Shade has a youthfully ripped body— all tan and fit and flexible. It's more beautiful than Rick the Dick ever was. Ugh. I cringe. Note to self: I can't think about Rick the Dick if I don't want my vag to implode on itself.

I focus on Shade again. I imagine what he would look like poised above me as he guides his enormous, perfect young penis into me. I imagine him sucking my nipples and pulling my hair in ecstasy as he pounds me like a bass drum at a Kiss concert.

I move Geronimo just a bit more.

Then a bit more.

And just like that, I come.

Merry Christmas to me.

As I lay in stunned, breathless satisfaction, I seriously think of texting Sara with my eternal gratitude.

Holy shit, girl! I think I love you.

Actually, I'm in love with Geronimo.

It's the perfect penis: Huge, hard and unattached to the rest of a man who would only bring problems like a beer gut, hellacious gas and infidelity. I gaze at it fondly as I wash it again, then tuck it into my bedside stand.

Yep, I'm definitely in love.

With a happy sigh, I realize that for the first time, I'm looking forward to my date on Saturday night.

****

"You look marvelous!" Sara says when I round the corner into the bedroom.

"I feel ridiculous."

"Why? We are simply two wealthy women with trophy boy toys out for a night on the town at one of Vegas's most luxurious night spots. Nothing to feel ridiculous about."

"I'm dressed like Julia Roberts in *Pretty Woman*, only without the body for it," I say, indicating my short, tight dress. "How did I let you talk me into buying this?"

"Well, I thought it might help things with Rick the Dick many moons ago, but this is an even better use. Besides, you look mouthwatering. You do too have the body for it."

Standing up, she walks to me. She trails the fingertips of one hand down my cheek before she rakes her long fingernails through my hair.

"Such great hair," she murmurs. "It's a perfect dark color and it's so shiny and full. You could be on a shampoo commercial. Seriously." I roll my eyes and smile, but she interrupts me before I can even speak. "And your teeth!" she observes. "You've got perfect teeth. Blindingly white. Your smile almost makes me hate you. What man can resist that?"

I stare at her incredulously. "My teeth? What the hell? No man is going to date me on the merits of my oral health. I'm not a horse, Sara."

"And such a beautiful face," she continues, ignoring me. Right before she drags her hands down to palm my boobs next. She gives them a squeeze.

"Delicious rack," she declares, then grabs my waist and spins me around. "And a perfect ass," she exclaims, slapping my butt. "You are gorgeous in every way and any man in his right mind would give his left nut to lick you from head to toe and everywhere in between."

"I think you secretly have the hots for me," I laugh. "Maybe I should be going out with you instead."

"Oh, you flatter! If either of us swung that way, we'd be perfect together. But, alas, I'm a sausage lover, as are you. No tacos for us."

I can't help but laugh. "Have you always been this way and I'm just now noticing?"

"Yes. You've been preoccupied for a few years."

"I'm beginning to really love this new you. Even if she shocks me regularly and gets me into trouble more often than not."

"You love it and you know it. I add much-needed excitement to your life," Sara claims, walking to the mirror to touch up her lipstick.

"Did I tell you I love that hair style on you, too?" I ask, referring to her new dark red pixie cut. She totally has the face to pull it off.

"Keep going like that and I'm yours."

We both laugh.

"Well, I guess I'm ready." I add under my breath, "At least as ready as I'll ever be."

"Then it's time to go."

My stomach flutters in dread and anxiety and, yes, a little bit of excitement. I take a deep breath and smile at Sara. She loops her arms through mine and grins.

"Welcome to the first night of the rest of your life."

We make our way outside and down the walk to the curb, to the shiny black limousine waiting there. The ride is only twenty minutes or so, during which I drink champagne in the back of the limo at a rate of speed that would make a sailor proud.

When we glide to a stop at the club, I follow Sara out of the car.

And the man waiting for me nearly takes my breath away.

He's taller than I imagined and much broader than I expected. His shoulders look a mile wide in his perfectly-tailored tuxedo, making his waist look smaller than mine. His hair is dark brown and his eyes are the same dark, sparkling blue as they are in his picture.

He's young, all right. But there is nothing boyish about this guy. Not at all.

As I step from the car, he extends his hand toward me. I slip my fingers into his and he smiles. I'm pretty sure my knees go numb and my uterus has a spasm. But it's when he speaks that I know it's all over but the shouting. And the Hallelujah choir.

"You're more beautiful than I could've imagined," he purrs in a deep, velvety voice.

Yep, I'm gonna ride him like a runaway bull tonight. No two ways about it.

The thought makes me smile.

Chapter Two

(Because sometimes you just gotta have the guy's perspective)

Shade

"You're a rock star," I mutter to the guy in the mirror as I tug his black tie into a crisp bow. "A fucking rock star."

"Dude, who the hell are you talking to?"

Chaz strides into the dressing room.

Correction. Chaz struts into the room. Chaz struts into every room like a little rooster. It's annoying as hell. In fact, *he's* annoying as hell. But since two women requested us both together, we're stuck with each other tonight. And I know that he doesn't like it any more than I do. He's an asshole and I just pray that I can get through the night without knocking his teeth down the back of his cocky little rooster throat.

I don't answer. I just return my attention to the man in the mirror. The guy staring back at me is confident, worldly and sexy as hell. He's comfortable in the starched penguin suit and he can charm a woman's Victoria Secret panties right off of her.

He's Shade. And Shade is a fucking rockstar.

"You about ready?" Chaz cocks an eyebrow at me and waits impatiently. "You're such a fucking girl," he mutters beneath his breath.

I glance at him. He's sitting on a red velvet lounge to my left, his short legs thumping restlessly against the wooden legs. He's just a short little guy. I don't see what women see in him. As he waits, he grabs a mint from the silver dish beside him and plunks it into his mouth, adhering to one of our rules. *Always have fresh breath, but never chomp on gum.*

This dressing room is plush, quiet and meant to be calming. Most of my colleagues (and I use that term loosely) don't need to be calmed. They've been doing this for quite a while. I'm the new kid on the block, the youngest and newest on the team. I've only been doing this for six months, but I've done it every weekend, which makes twenty four weekends of this. Of *dates.*

That's what we call them. Dates.

I smile to myself because dates in high school or even college were never like this. The vague memory of clutching and groping at each other in parked cars in dark alleys with fogged up car windows comes to mind and I almost laugh.

My life has certainly progressed.

Ever since my friend Adam introduced me to this job, my life has changed for the better. I no longer have to beg money from my old man and live by his rules. I can pay my own way because I make a LOT of money by doing something that I love. And that means that I don't have to get the freaking business degree that my father wanted me to get. I have no interest in that. I don't really know what I'm interested in yet, but it's sure as hell not business.

The man in the mirror smiles at me, confident and ready. He's 6'1" and his dark hair is tousled. He shakes it out of the way to reveal his dark blue eyes. Cobalt, some women have called them. Whatever the fuck that is. Whatever it is, I'm good with it. They seem to like it.

"Ready," the man in the mirror says and I turn to face Chaz.

I'm Shade now. And Shade is ready for anything. Anytime, anywhere.

I grab a mint on the way out.

I'm a fucking rockstar.

We make our way down the back halls of Utopia. Only customers paying the high escort prices will ever see these halls and the rooms adjoined to them. It still astounds me that women would pay that sort of money just to have sex with a man. I mean, hell. Women can always get it if they want it. They don't have to pay for it.

Yet these women do. They hand over their credit cards without blinking, simply because they want to have no-strings-tied sex with me. They like getting to tell me exactly what they want and knowing that I won't judge them for it.

Even though there is some freaky, kinky shit going on here. Stuff I never even knew existed until I came to work here.

I adjust my jacket as I walk past the closed doors. I don't hear anything from behind them. The doors and walls are thick here for a reason.

Complete anonymity. Utopia promises that to its patrons. The women who walk through these halls must wear a velvet blindfold until they are safely ensconced in a bedroom with a closed door. It protects the identity of them and of anyone else that they might see.

The halls are red with textured wallpaper. The wall sconces are dimly lit and it creates a seductive atmosphere, even though the patrons never see these particular walls. I walk through with ease now. I'm Shade. And Shade never gets nervous.

We reach the doors that lead out to the main club, the normal face of Utopia. Normal people who just want to drink and dance are out there, dancing like fools on the dance floor with their neon green wristbands flashing in the dark. The guards who stand at each side of the back hallway know not to let anyone wearing a green wrist band in. Of course, no one without an escort can get in, period.

It's very exclusive.

And that makes *me* very exclusive. I straighten my shoulders. When I am here, inside the walls of Utopia, I act differently. I know no fear, I have no boundaries. I am always up for anything.

I am always hard, always ready. It's what they pay me for.

We make our way through the throngs of sweaty people and come out of the front doors just in time to find two women getting out of shiny black limo. At first, all I can see are slender legs. The woman that they are attached to spreads them slightly before she climbs out, purposely giving us a clear shot of her bare crotch.

Classy.

She's skinny and pale with a strikingly short fire-engine red hair cut. She's rich and she's definitely used to commanding attention. I can tell that from here. She's fine to look at, but honestly, I find my attention captured by the beautiful woman climbing out behind her.

Sweet Jesus.

It's at times like this that I truly, truly love my job.

I offer her my hand, helping her from the car.

She's fairly tall for a chick, and slender, but she's got womanly hips and a perfect rack. She's wearing a short, barely there skirt and a shirt that perfectly shows off her lush, full cleavage.

I wasn't expecting this when they told me that my client tonight was in her mid-thirties. This woman has a tight, tight body. She must work out. Dark brown hair curls around her shoulders and from the way she is staring, I know she is here for me.

Thank you, God.

"You're more beautiful than I could've imagined," I tell her. And I mean it. She looks instantly more relaxed as a small smile curves her lips.

"Shade?" she asks, her voice fairly quiet. She's hesitant, nothing at all like her bordering-on-obnoxious friend. I bend to kiss her hand. That's another rule. *Always pamper your date.*

They certainly pay a high premium for it.

She smiles and the darkness around us lights up.

I smile back.

"I'm Shade," I confirm. "And you must be Allison."

"You can call me Alli," she says. I can see she's nervous. Another rule: Always make your date comfortable.

"Well, Alli," I tell her with a confident grin, "Welcome to the best night of your life."

She smiles back radiantly, but I can still see a little of her shyness lurking there. It's charming and I hold my arm out.

"Shall we?" I ask.

She nods, her lips tightening just a bit. She's definitely nervous.

As we walk, I lean in, my lips grazing the sensitive skin by her ear. She smells of a classy perfume. I don't know what it is. Whatever it is, it makes me want to lick her.

"Relax," I murmur to her. "You're going to enjoy yourself. I promise."

She looks at me, her hazel eyes meeting mine.

"I have no doubt."

We thread our way through the thumping, noisy club. Allison's fingers are resting lightly on my arm and I guide her through the crowds. When we get to the private back hallway, Chaz and his date stop while he blind-folds her. She waggles her fingers at Allison, calling "Enjoy yourself, love!" over her shoulder.

I turn to Allison with the blindfold in my hand.

"Is that really necessary?" she asks uncertainly.

"What?" I ask. "Blindfolding you?" She nods and I step behind her.

I trail my fingers over the skin of her breasts slightly. She sucks in her breath and I lean in once again to whisper in her ear. "Trust me. You'll like it."

I tug the blindfold until it is tight, then wrap her fingers once again around my arm as I lead her through the halls and to a private room.

This is going to be fun.

Chapter Three

(Or: Am I Really Freaking Doing This?)

Alli

Holy freaking Hell.

I'm internally having a panic attack because I've never been blind-folded before. And here I am, letting a beautiful gigolo blindfold me and lead me away to his sex nest.

"Breathe, Allison," the beautiful gigolo tells me in my ear. His voice is husky and rich, like hot caramel or warm maple syrup...or even better, like melted chocolate. I swallow, instantly hungry and turned on at the same time.

"Okay," I agree, trying to force my traitorous lungs to fill with air.

They are having none of it though and I gasp like an idiot, even though the blindfold is velvet and satin. It's hardly uncomfortable, but it still makes me anxious. What is waiting for me that he needs to blind me for? Weird whips and chains? Hand cuffs and ben wah balls?

Holy freaking hell.

I am practically panting when I hear a door being unlocked with the swipe of a card. I hear it click and then a doorknob turning. Then I am being gently pulled into the sex nest.

Oh my god.

Oh my god.

What have I done?

I'm in a freaking sex nest!

I'm too old for this shit.

Then the blindfold is taken off.

And I am surrounded by luxury. By heavy, expensive furniture. By thick and cushiony duvet covers and pillows. By opulent decorations in crystal and mahogany. By sheer normalcy in this room.

Sheer.

Freaking.

Normalcy.

I'm shocked.

And I must look it, because Shade turns to me and laughs.

"What?" he grins. "Were you expecting something else?"

"Yes," I admit. "I don't know what. But not this."

"Perhaps this?" Shade suggests and pushes a button on the wall. A door on the ceiling slides silently open and a sex swing drops down, dangling at the edge of the bed.

I gulp as I realize that it looks like a noose… a noose that I'm probably going to hang myself with.

"Maybe," I answer.

I examine it closer. It's terrifying. It looks like a contraption of torture, like something out of Morticia and Gomez Addams' bedroom. The harness is lined with cushiony velvet. But it still doesn't look comfortable. And maybe not even legal. I gulp again.

Shade laughs again.

"Nervous?"

I nod.

"Don't be," he tells me, his voice buttery smooth. He moves closer to me and I unconsciously step back. He grins again. And I suddenly feel like a lion and its prey. "We don't have to use it. Yet."

Shade throws back his head and laughs and I am once again reminded that I am the visitor here. I am the prey, he is the lion. This is his stomping ground, his Serengeti. He knows what he's doing and I don't, even though I'm almost twenty years older than he is. Probably.

I narrow my eyes.

"How old are you?" I ask.

Shade stops laughing and examines me.

"Oh, now, Alli," he murmurs, taking a step toward me. "Age is just a number, you know. I promise you that tonight, my age or even your age, will be the last thing on your mind. In fact, hopefully, when I'm finished with you, you're going to have a hard time remembering your own name."

I have to smile at that, right after I pant for a second. But I gain control, turn to Shade and grin what I hope is a calm and confident grin.

"Oh, really? You're that sure of yourself?"

Shade shrugs. "I have to be. If you don't believe in yourself, no one else will do it for you."

"That's a good point," I nod. "Very mature."

"I'm very, very mature. Now come here," he instructs. "Tell me what you'd like."

My heart pounds so loudly that I'm sure he can hear it from there. Hell, Canada can probably hear it. I blink hard then take a step.

"I was married for fifteen years to a guy who was luke-warm in bed at best. I honestly don't know what I like."

Shade puts one beautiful finger against his mouth, which is also beautiful, and appraises me silently for a moment.

"Hmm," he finally says, his cobalt eyes twinkling. "It sounds like you need me to show you want you want. And you're in luck. Because here at Utopia, we have a 100% Customer Satisfaction policy. That means that I must do everything in my power to make sure you're satisfied. In every way."

Shade stares at me, his gaze intense and sexy and mind-blowing.

He takes a step forward.

I take a step back.

Lion and prey.

Lion and prey.

I'm like a little wounded gazelle.

In stilettos.

And that means that I can't run.

Fuck.

I pant again.

"You're fine," Shade assures me softly, watching me and appraising me while probably plotting how to capture me. "Why don't you sit on the bed—I'll be back in a second."

He turns around and steps into a room that I didn't notice before. It has to be the bathroom. He pokes his head back around the corner.

"And you might want to make yourself comfortable."

He's gone again.

Make myself comfortable?

What does he mean by that?

Take my clothes off??

Good Lord. I glance down at my outfit which feels like it has shrunk two sizes in the last two minutes- probably due to the fact that I can't seem to breathe. I probably shouldn't have worn shapewear that is thick enough to hold in a middle-aged guy's beer gut.

Holy shit.

The shapewear.

Why did I wear freaking shapewear??

I scramble to get it off. I can't have beautiful and perfect Shade undress me and find this hideous beige undergarment. I'd be too humiliated to ever look at him again, much less orgasm under his very skilled fingers.

And I'm just guessing about that last part- but I'm certain that he's skilled.

He's a professional, after all.

Did I mention HOLY SHIT?

I fly into motion and kick off my stilettos so that I can unpeel the fricking shapewear from my mildly damp torso. I can't believe I'm sweating. I'm sure that the perfect and gorgeous Shade never sweats. And all the thinking about sweating makes me wonder if I smell.

Hell.

I'm just lifting an arm to do a quick whiff test, when Shade comes walking out of the bathroom.

Oh, freaking perfect.

He grins and acts as though he doesn't notice that one of my arms is in the air, my nose is buried in it and the other arm is caught half-way through the tight armhole of my industrial-strength-glorified-girdle.

Sweet Jesus.

And Shade's tuxedo is gone now. He's wearing only the black slacks. His chest is bare and sculpted and perfect. And rippled. And it sort of glistens in the soft light. OhMyWord. I instantly want to lick it.

Holy Freaking Hell.

Shade saunters over to me and gently grabs my wrist, the one that is attached to the arm in the air, and lowers that seemingly paralyzed arm for me. As he does, he slides his nose along the skin of my forearm.

"You smell delicious," he tells me.

I want to melt into the floor. Both because he knows what I was doing and because his voice is so to-die-for-sexy. I look at him and he stares back unapologetically.

"Don't be self-conscious," he instructs me calmly. "About anything. That's rule number one. All inhibitions should be left at that door in order for you to have the most fulfilling experience possible."

"All of them?" I ask, thinking about my flying squirrel arms. Shade nods.

"All of them."

"And there are rules?" I ask, somewhat nervous about that fact. I wasn't shown a rule-book.

"Only a few." He peels my thick elastic underwear down and I step out of it. He throws it into the corner of the room with a disgusted look on his face.

"Rule number two: Don't wear that ridiculous shit again. You don't need it."

He looks down at me, his gaze appreciative as he runs his fingers along my newly bared torso. Goosebumps form where ever he touches.

"You're perfect."

"I'm paying you, so of course you're going to say that," I point out. He smiles, a grin full of mischief and cockiness.

"True. But I'm always honest," he tells me. "Always."

And then he shoves me onto the bed.

I go flying, sprawled unceremoniously on the thick cushiony duvet.

"What the hell?" I sputter. And then I am instantly overwhelmed again by the beauty of his rippled chest as he climbs onto the bed, like an agile jungle cat, toward me...up and over me. I feel slightly overpowered. I sort of like the feeling.

"You need someone to show you who is boss," he says seriously. "I think I have you pegged, Alli. You've been the caretaker, the decision-maker and the wonder woman for too long. You need someone to make the decisions and to take care of you."

"You've gathered all of this in ten minutes?" I ask, not wanting to acknowledge that he is 100% correct.

He nods. "You're easy to read."

Shade moves with all the agility of a leopard as he positions himself above me, the skin of his forearm pressed against the skin of my side. I try not to hyperventilate as I stare into his blue, blue, blue freaking eyes.

"And I'm going to take care of you," he promises. "Every inch of you."

Oh. My. God.

I can't breathe.

Shade dips his head and without any preamble at all, he buries his face in my cleavage as he reaches beneath me and unsnaps my black lacy bra. And then he discards it next to the bed and licks a circle around my nipple.

"Ah!" I cry out and grab the pillows next to me. Shade smiles against the skin of my breast, his mouth widening, moving... then sucking.

"Oh my god," I can't help but whisper. It's like every nerve ending in my entire body is on fire right now- on def-con-five hyper alert and actually, they might implode. Or explode. Or whatever it is that over-charged nerve endings do. I might stroke out, actually.

I gather my courage and release the pillows, instead stroking the silky skin of Shade's young and muscular back. Holy hell. Rick the Dick was never built like this- not even in his prime. Not even in his *dreams* when he was in his prime.

Must not think of Rick the dick.

Must not think of Rick the dick, I chant silently. But honestly, it's not something I have to repeat for long. My attention is focused solely on this perfection in front of me.

And then, before I can trail my fingers down to Shade's perfectly chiseled ass, he is grasping both of my wrists in his hand and clamping handcuffs on each one, binding me to the headboard.

What the hell?

I look at him in alarm.

He stares back calmly.

"Allison, you've been a caretaker for too long. Tonight, I'm going to take care of you. But I'm afraid that if I don't restrain you, you're going to try and focus on taking care of me. Trust me, I've got that. Before the night is over, you're going to scream my name- many times over. But if at any point you want me to stop or you want these handcuffs taken off, then I want you to yell out *pineapple*."

I stare at him. "Pineapple? Why?"

"Because it's something I like to eat," he shrugs. "Are your handcuffs too tight?"

I wiggle my wrists, testing them. The padding on the metal is thick and comfortable. So I shake my head. "No."

"Do you trust me?" Shade smiles. His smile is sort of wicked. And I sort of like it. It makes me feel sort of wicked, too.

"Yes," I answer. I don't know why, but I do. He wouldn't have repeat customers if he wasn't trustworthy, right? I nod for emphasis.

"Good. Is there anything that you absolutely do not want me to do?"

I think on that. Well, I think on that as well as I can with him balanced above me. He's slightly distracting.

"I don't think so," I finally say. "I don't know of anything that I already know that I hate. If you do something, I'll tell you. Deal?"

"Deal," he grins. I'm in love with his grin. I want to find a luxury apartment in SoHo or some equally cool neighborhood and co-habitate with it and have its little grin babies. That's how much I love it.

Shade palms my ribs with his large hands, the warmth of them erasing the goose-bumps that had formed there. He grasps my sides and pulls me up, arching my back. Staring into my eyes, he bends his head and licks a circle around my belly-button. His tongue is warm and soft. In fact, it's probably the only soft thing on his entire body. Except for his hair. He has great hair. And why am I thinking about his hair?

He drags his tongue in a trail up my abdomen towards my breasts, but instead of stopping there like I expected, he continues to my neck. He nuzzles it, then kisses it. Then licks it. Then sucks it. I am moaning by this time. Who knew that the neck was such an erogenous zone? Holy cow.

He moves to my ear and pays the same attention there, then continues to my mouth. By this time, I am ready for his kiss. I want his tongue in me. Anywhere in me. But right now, I'll settle for his mouth. His mouth crushes mine, in a kiss that is not gentle, but it is certainly consuming. I can't breathe by the time his tongue is finished exploring mine.

"Do you trust me?" he asks again, staring into my eyes. I feel flushed and hot and disheveled. I nod.

"Yes."

"Good. I'm going to blindfold you again. And you're going to like it."

I nod. "Yes. I think I will."

Shade laughs, a low chuckle. "I *know* you will."

He pulls the blindfold over my eyes and the room goes black. I am instantly remorseful of only one thing. I can no longer stare at Shade. That's regretful, for sure. I can't stare at him and I can't touch him. I'm not so sure about this blindfold business.

Until he starts lapping at my inner right thigh.

My heart pounds in time with his tongue.

"You have exquisite legs," he says softly. "You must work out."

I can't answer because I am busy panting.

I feel so completely dominated right now — blindfolded, handcuffed. And for some reason, it feels liberating too. I'm trusting this person enough to explore this with him. And I might be crazy. But I love it.

But not as much as I'm about to.

His mouth covers my clit, his lips closing around it like a vacuum.

And my hips instantly and with a mind of their own, buck against him.

"You like that, little kitten?" he murmurs. And then he starts licking. And then there's a finger involved, sliding in and out and holy-freaking-damnation. What have I been missing out on for the entire rest of my life prior to this moment?

I am soaking wet now. I can feel the liquid, the moisture, pooling between my legs, but he licks it away; lap, lap, lapping. And I am riding exquisite waves of something awesome. That is the only way to describe it. All of those stupid romance novels that I used to read that described orgasms as riding waves of pleasure? They were so freaking right. And to think that I'd stopped reading them because I thought they were unrealistic.

"You're so tight, Alli Cat," Shade whispers, sliding his finger in me. At the same time, he is finessing me with his tongue. And I might seriously die. And I love that he just called me Alli Cat.

"Hold your breath for a minute," he instructs me. "You're going to come. And it will make it better."

I do as he says.

And he's right. I come in the next moment and holding my breath made it better.

I release a shaky exhale, falling limp against the bed.

And then without warning or any kind of clue whatsoever, other than a brief metallic rustling of foil, Shade is sliding into me. His penis is thick and long and full and I gasp. I wish I could clutch him and hold on, but my arms are still secured to the bed. So I lock my legs around him and pull him as close as I can.

Shade smells heavenly, like fresh air and male and cedar. I inhale him as he rides me. He slides in and out quickly, then he slows down. Then he speeds up. Then he slows down. It's excruciatingly exquisite.

He freezes, hovering with the tip of his penis at the apex of my thighs.

"Say you like my cock," he tells me, his voice hot in my ear. The word is so naughty and I've honestly never said it out loud. But I don't hesitate now.

"I like your cock," I tell him.

"Say you fucking love my cock," he answers. His breathing is just a bit ragged.

"I fucking love your cock," I whisper.

He rams into me; hard, harder, harder.

"Scream it," he instructs raggedly.

So I do. And it feels liberating. I always felt so repressed, so self-conscious with my ex-husband. Screaming obscenities while a beautiful man fucks me feels amazing. So I do it again. And again. And again.

Shade was right. By the end of the evening, in fact, by only halfway through the evening, I am screaming his name.

Chapter Four

(Or: Another glimpse into Shade's Male Mind)

Shade
Allison's body is tight and hot and nothing like I expected. But then, I've come to realize that nothing in this line of work is ever what I should expect.

And for that, I should be thankful.

I'm going to fuck Allison into the wee hours of the night.

And for that, I know she will be thankful.

End cohesive thought here as all blood is diverted away from the brain and into the male head that is not capable of significant thought

Chapter Five

(Or: It's a Great Day for an Attempted Murder)

Alli

I wake up feeling....satisfied.

Since it is Saturday, I don't have to roll out of bed and rush to the shower in a bleary-eyed haze. I lie still and lazy, staring up at the ceiling, remembering last night.

Holy. Shizz.

Memories of Shade's lips trailing over my entire body fill up my mind. His fingers were everywhere, fondling, touching, pulling, kneading.

I gulp.

I never ever *ever* knew that fucking could be like that. And it was fucking. You can't call it making love when there was no love involved. But it was soft and sensuous, then hard and rough, then soft again. I swallow hard, my fingers touching my neck. At one point, after Shade released my handcuffs, he fucked me from behind and held me in place by the back of my neck.

It was hard and rough and primal.

And I liked it.

What is wrong with me??

I push off the covers and step over my going-out clothes that I had discarded on the floor. I slept naked for the first time in a very long time. Actually, make that ever.

There is nothing wrong with me, I decide as I stare into the mirror and brush my teeth.

I'm a healthy, red-blooded female. I like sex. I have every right to explore this new side of me. .I scrub my teeth vigorously as I debate internally with my conscious.

I don't need to feel guilty. I did nothing wrong.

I glare at myself and then spit.

And then as I straighten back up, Sophie's alarmed face is behind me in the mirror.

"Mom! Geez! Put some clothes on. God!"

She turns away as she slaps a hand over her eyes and I feel blood rushing to my cheeks while I reach for a robe.

"I'm sorry, Soph. I didn't know you were back so soon. Wait. Why am I apologizing? It's my bathroom. If you knocked first, you wouldn't be surprised."

I paste a nonchalant look on my face and turn around.

Sophie is staring at me.

"Where did you go last night wearing those shoes?"

She points to my pile of discarded clothing.

"Oh. Sara and I just went out dancing last night. We needed to blow off some steam. Did you have fun at your dad's? Why are you home so early? I thought you weren't coming home until tomorrow."

Rick doesn't take her for his weekends as often as he can. In fact, he rarely does. And Sophie does a good job of acting like she doesn't care. But I know she does. And it makes me want to put those stilettos back on and march

over to his freaking condo and impale him squarely in the
ass.

Sophie sighs, bringing me back to the present and
away from my murderous thoughts.

"Daddy had to work today, apparently. I didn't want
to sit in his condo all day because there's nothing to do
there. So I asked him to bring me here on his way to work.
Was that okay? He's going to pick me back up on his way
home."

She's looking at me worriedly and I rush to reassure
her, even though I don't relish the thought of seeing Rick
today. In fact, a little bile rises up in my throat, sour and
acidic. But I swallow it and nod.

"Of course, sweetie. That's fine. I'm always glad to
have you home."

Her face is instantly relieved and then slips once more
into the self-assured teen that she is.

"I thought maybe we could go shopping today, if you
don't have anything to do. We can have a
mother/daughter day. I need some black jeans. What do
you think?"

I scrunch up my nose as I dig through my dresser
drawer for my own jeans.

"Hmm. It depends. If they aren't $400 jeans, then
maybe. If they are, then you need to ask your dad."

Sophie laughs, as though she'd never ask me to buy
something so ridiculous. We both know that isn't the case.

"Please, mom. We can have lunch too. And maybe
get our nails done."

I sigh. I can literally feel the money flying out of my
wallet as we speak. But I love my daughter. And as usual,

when she wants something, I have a really hard time saying no.

"Fine," I sigh, as I reach for my favorite stretched out, faded sweatshirt. It's the one that I've had since college and long ago cut the collar out so that it hangs off my shoulders. It's as old as the hills and does nothing for my figure, but I love it in spite of that fact.

"Fine," I repeat. "I needed some moisturizer anyway."

"Are you wearing that?" Sophie eyes me doubtfully.

"Don't push it," I raise an eyebrow. She rolls her eyes before ducking out and I finish getting ready by pulling my hair into a low ponytail and sliding on some lip-gloss. I don't have anyone to impress today, right? I can wear what I want to, even if it is a public mall.

If I'm going to be spending god only knows how much money on my daughter's endless wardrobe needs, I deserve to wear my favorite sweatshirt.

****

I regret the sweatshirt within two hours of putting it on.

Being wrapped up in the afterglow of great sex with someone twenty years younger than me, I had neglected to remember that it is Las Vegas in springtime. I don't need a sweatshirt. In fact, if I could walk around naked without going to jail for public indecency, I very well might.

But as it is, I am sweaty and grumpy as Sophie and I pile our purchases (all $793 dollars worth) in the trunk of my black Audi. To be fair, $234 dollars was used on me. The rest though, was Sophie.

"Thanks for the stuff, Mom," she says to me brightly before she sticks her ear-buds into her ears and forgets that I exist.

Seriously. The little snot actually turns toward the window and stares out, oblivious to my presence now that I have financed her little clothing habit. I shake my head. There are times, like right now, when I can totally understand why hamsters eat their young.

"You're welcome," I mutter as I push my stupid long sleeves up for the millioneth time and shove my over-heated face in front of the air-conditioning for a minute, in hopes of bringing my tomato-red cheeks down to a nice neutral shade of tan. Or at the very most, a becoming blush.

I glance down at the clock as I turn up the radio. It's only 1:30. We still have time for lunch before we need to be home for Rick to pick Sophie up.

I click the car into Reverse and am backing out just as a voice registers in my head.

"Yoo-hoo! Allison! Is that you?"

And then there's a sickening thud.

Hand to God- I didn't have time to react between hearing the voice and the sickening thud.

Sophie's eyes fly to meet mine and I slam on the brakes, throw the car into park and we jump out of the car to find a nauseatingly thin crumpled heap directly behind my left back tire.

And I say nauseatingly thin because I know exactly who it is. I can tell from her cheap sense of style and the giant rock on her left spidery ring finger.

It's Rick's new fiancée, Vanessa.

And she's nauseatingly thin.

Except for her fake boobs, which Rick bought and paid for and can be used as flotation devices in the unlikely event of a plane crash. Apparently though, they don't work very well in the more likely event of an automobile vs. pedestrian crash.

I gasp as I drop to my knees beside her.

"Vanessa! Oh my god! Are you alright! Can you hear me?!"

She moans and turns to look at me, whimpering pitifully.

"Do you hate me this much, Allison? Really?"

I stare at her, at her perfect baby blue eyes, her perfectly sculpted eyebrows, her Barbie-like twenty-three year old perfect body and her full, pouty candy-apple-pink lips. Yes, yes, I hate her. But she's not worth going to jail for. Even though I might have fantasized about it a few times. I'm not gonna lie.

"I didn't see you, Vanessa," I sigh. "Why were you behind my car?"

"Why didn't you watch where you were going?" she snaps as she studies a candy-apple-pink fingernail. Her polish perfectly matches her lips. "I just had my nails done and this one is broken. Thanks a lot."

I sigh again, offering her my hand.

"Are you hurt?" I ask. Sophie is hovering over my shoulder. She has yanked her ear-buds out for this bit of excitement. Vanessa shakes her head.

"I don't think so. Except for my nail. You're paying to get it fixed, Allison!" she snaps again. "I was only coming over to say hello and you ran me down like a lunatic."

"I didn't run you down," I say tiredly as I haul her to her feet. "I just didn't see—"

I am interrupted by Miss Perfect's cry of pain. And then distracted by her rabid hopping on one thin leg. I briefly wonder if the spindly little thing has just collapsed under her weight, before I realize that is ridiculous. Her body weight couldn't collapse a piece of wet toilet paper.

"Ow, ow, ow!!! I think my foot is broken. You broke my foot, you vicious bitch!" Vanessa has abandoned her pretense of being the coy wounded child.

I am startled and look down at her stiletto clad foot. Who wears stilettos to the mall on a Saturday morning, anyway?

Her ankle is turning purple- I can see it from here.

"I bet you twisted it when you fell," I tell her, putting my arm under her shoulder to help support her. "Why are you wearing heels?"

Vanessa glares at me. "This has nothing to do with my shoes, so don't even try to blame me. You ran me down."

I sigh again. If there was something sharp near me, I would grab it and poke my eyes out.

"I didn't run you down," I tell her again. "I merely backed into you. But we should probably get you to the doctor to look at your foot. Are you with anyone?"

I glance behind her but don't see anyone. And she shakes her head.

"No. You're going to have to take me. It's the least you can do, anyway."

"Yes, it's the least I can do." I level a gaze at her as I practically shove her into my backseat. "Watch your head."

I look at Sophie. "Soph, call your father and tell him to meet us at the Desert Springs Medical Center. They have an urgent care center."

She nods and pulls her phone out and I concentrate on tuning out Vanessa's whining, moaning and outright bitchy accusations.

"You're not taking me there. It's a deathtrap for bums and people on welfare."

"You just wanted to disfigure me so that Rick won't want me anymore."

"You're just jealous because I'm younger and hotter than you."

I don't bother to reply to any of it and it's a very long twenty minute drive, but luckily Sophie has turned her music back on and doesn't hear anything.

When we finally reach the medical center, I have Sophie run up and get a wheelchair and then I wheel Vanessa in myself. I am feeling rather cocky that I am able to resist the urge to steer her directly into the path of a utility van that careens through the parking lot.

Must not kill Vanessa.

Must not kill Vanessa.

Must not kill Vanessa.

I chant this silently in my head as we enter the sliding doors and get her checked in. I am just trying to decide whether to leave her alone or not when Rick struts through the waiting room doors.

Rick struts everywhere because he feels that nothing starts until he arrives.

My ex-husband is not bad looking. As far as thirty-nine year old men go, he's pretty hot. He's around six feet tall and has dark hair with just the beginning of silver at his temples. He's clean shaven and he works out. He owns his own ad company, which is where he met Vanessa. She was his administrative assistant. Apparently she was *very* good at 'assisting' him.

But I digress.

On the surface, Rick's a catch. He's good-looking and successful. But what you can't tell from looking at him is that he is a cheating, lying worm. And I instantly remember that I should feel sorry for Vanessa rather than hate her. She has no idea what she's getting herself into. Although the gold-digging whore probably deserves it.

Holy crap! Did I say that out loud?? I look around quickly and breathe a sigh of relief. Thank god. I didn't.

"What the hell have you done?" Rick snaps at me as he approaches us. He doesn't care that we are in the middle of a crowded waiting room or that his daughter is standing with me.

"Nothing. Your girlfriend stepped behind my car while I was backing out," I answer firmly.

"Bull shit," Rick barks. He reaches us and bends down to kiss Vanessa on the lips and strokes her platinum blonde hair.

"Are you alright, pumpkin?" he croons to her and I seriously fight the urge to vomit. Pumpkin? What is she? Twelve? Oh, wait. She is. Or she might as well be.

She shows him her broken fingernail and her swollen foot and whimpers pathetically.

Rick straightens up and turns back to me.

"Are you satisfied?" he demands. "You wanted to get back at me and now you have. But you didn't have to assault Vanessa to do it."

"Rick, that's ridiculous—" I begin.

"Dad," Sophie interrupts. "I was there. Mom didn't do it on purpose. Vanessa stepped behind our car. It was an accident."

Rick whirls around, glaring at her. "Sophie, stay out of this. Your mother has done a terrible thing. I can't believe that you would defend her."

I stare at him incredulously.

"A terrible thing? If, by terrible, you mean that I picked your teeny-bopper girlfriend off of the pavement after she stepped in front of my already-moving vehicle and twisted her ankle because she was wearing stilts to go shopping in, before I practically carried her to my backseat and drove her across town to the hospital where I got her checked in and settled into the waiting room to wait for you... then yes, you're right. I did a terrible thing. If you meant anything else, then you're insane. Have a good day, Rick."

I brush past him and start to walk away and he calls from behind me.

"Look forward to hearing from our lawyer. You're going to have a lawsuit on your hands for this."

I am startled and freeze. I count to five and take deep breaths so that I don't turn around and kill them both. I turn slowly while silently applauding my Herculean restraint.

"Rick, you're an idiot. There are video cameras in the mall parking lot. I am certain that any jury or judge in America would decide that I didn't do anything wrong. They will see your girlfriend step behind me and will see that it was an accident. They will also see that your girlfriend is practically a child, so every female on the jury will agree with me anyway, just on principle. But if you want to pursue it, then by all means do so. Whatever floats your boat, because we both know that you're having some problems in that area."

Oh, burn! The look on Rick's face is priceless. And I should feel guilty for saying those things in front of Sophie, but I'm too mad to think clearly. I turn to leave and Sophie joins me.

I look at her in surprise as Rick demands that she stay. She turns to him.

"I changed my mind, dad. I don't want to spend the weekend with you. Not until you learn to treat mom better."

She turns on her heel and walks for the car. I am stunned. Stupefied. Speechless.

"Oh, perfect. Now look what you've done," Rick sneers. "You've turned my daughter against me."

I'm stunned again and speechless. This is a record for me. Twice in one minute.

"Rick, you did that all on your own."

I turn on my own heel. I'm only regretful of one thing and that is wearing this stupid sweatshirt. It would be nice if I looked hot as hell in this moment, instead of frumpy and overheated. But oh well. There's nothing to be done for it.

I meet Sophie at my car.

She's got her ear-buds back in. I get in and turn to her, reaching over and pulling one ear-bud out.

"Sophie, you don't have to take sides. Your dad is your dad and I'm your mom. Our issues aren't your issues."

She looks at me like I've suddenly grown two heads and have begun wearing her cast-off clothing from last year.

"Are you insane?" she asks, her voice high-pitched. "Dad was being a dick. And I don't like being around dicks."

I automatically start to tell her not to call her father a dick. But he is being a dick. And we might as well call a dick a dick. So I shut my mouth and simply turn the car for home.

"Aren't we going to lunch?" Sophie pipes up, lifting her head from the passenger window.

"Seriously? After all of that, you're still thinking of food?"

She stares at me blankly. I sigh.

"You're such a teenager."

She smiles. "But I'm *your* teenager."

She knows exactly how to make me melt. She's a wily one, my daughter.

I take her to our favorite Chinese place where we gorge ourselves on Kung Pao chicken and then share a molten double chocolate volcano for dessert.

We are laughing by now and have completely forgotten about Rick the Dick's bad behavior.

"I'm just glad that Vanessa's fake boobs didn't pop," Sophie giggles as she takes a bite of chocolate sauce. "They would have felt that explosion all the way in Japan. It might have caused another Tsunami."

I can't help but laugh before I tell her not to joke about Tsunamis. She rolls her eyes.

"I'm not. I'm being serious. An explosion of that magnitude would probably trigger some sort of natural disaster somewhere. Maybe an avalanche in the Rockies or something. No lie."

I chuckle because she's right as I pay the bill. Vanessa's fake boobs are enormous.

"How big do you think they are?" I muse as I pull out my credit card. "D?"

Sophie's eyes light up wickedly. "They are DD's," she confirms. "I saw her tacky bra in the laundry at Dad's. I'm always waiting for her to fall over from the sheer weight of those things."

I know that I shouldn't joke around like this with Sophie, but after the morning we've had, I can't help but laugh with her. I know. Mom of the year, right here.

"Wanna go to a movie?" Sophie suggests as we leave. I stare at her in shock. She hasn't wanted to go to a movie with me in forever. I turned un-cool right about the time she turned thirteen. A total coincidence, I'm sure.

Sophie giggles as my mouth practically drops open.

"What?" she looks at me innocently. "It's a girl's day, isn't it?"

I melt again.

So, we go to a movie, share a giant tub of buttered popcorn and a vat of coke. Then we return home, pull on sweat pants and watch chick flicks all night.

As I lay curled up with my angelic-at-the-moment daughter, I ponder my state of current good luck.

All in all, I fucked an amazing younger sex god, ran down my cheating ex-husband's new fiancée (On accident!!) and had a spectacular girl's day with my sometimes-surly-but-not-today teen daughter. It was a fabulous fucking weekend.

Oh, and I forgot the fact that I have mastered the art of saying fuck.

Fuck, fuck, fuck, fuckity, fuck.

See? I'm getting good at it.

Chapter Six

(Or: When life throws you curve balls, fuck the
pitcher)

"I didn't return your calls yesterday because I was busy all
day. You know, plowing down Rick's fiancée in a parking
lot," I tell Sara as I chew on a pickle. She is picking apart
her sandwich in agitation. "Don't do that. You're going to
get ham under your fingernails."

Sara glares at me. "I heard you the first time you
explained it. And we'll get back to that because it's effing
hilarious. But first, I'm mad at you. Seriously. How hard
would it have been to simply call me back for just one
minute so that you could tell me how it went with Shade?
The whole thing was my idea. I deserve to hear all of the
juicy details."

I laugh. "Don't you mean you deserve to get off on all
the juicy details?"

She glares at me and I laugh again. She does have a
point.

"Okay, okay. Yes, I know. I owe you for this one.
Shade was fabulous."

Her eyes light up. "So, you *did* love riding the teenage
pony?"

I shudder.

"Shade is not a teenager."

She grins. "I know. But he's the closest legal thing."

"You're a sick, sick person, you know that?" I tell her. She nods without shame.

"I know. And for the record, I don't really want a teenager. I just like to be shocking."

"Don't I know it," I mutter.

"But that's neither here nor there," she announces with her fire-engine-red lips. "I only have thirty minutes left til I have to be back at the office. I have an open house this afternoon. I need to know. Was it amazing? Do you owe me a Lexus or a Ferrari?"

I grin. "Neither. But I do owe you a huge fucking thank you."

She squeals. "I knew it!! Tell me All. Of. It."

So I do. I tell her of the handcuffs, the rough sex, the licking, the biting, the....everything. She is staring dreamily into space as I finish up.

"I knew he'd be good," she tells me, drumming her red fingertips on the bistro table. "If I weren't so loyal to Chaz and so dedicated to ensuring that he gets a good college education, I might try Shade out."

"Ha! You don't care about his college tuition," I say, but I am shocked by how territorial I feel toward Shade and by how much I don't want him to have sex with Sara. I gulp. He's a gigolo. He has sex with a *lot* of people. That's what he does. It's his job. I gulp again.

"I do, too," Sara insists. "I am a true patron of the arts. Particularly interactive arts."

I giggle. "Sara, having sex is not an art."

She glares at me. "If you believe that, then you aren't doing it right. Speaking of doing it right, I made an appointment for you to go with me to get a Brazilian done day after tomorrow. You can thank me later. Or rather, Shade can." She laughs evilly. I stare at her, my mouth hanging open

"A Brazilian? As in, a Brazilian *wax*? Down *there*?"

My crotch is instantly terrified and tries to crawl inside of my body at my words.

I silently croon to it. *It's okay, my pet. I won't ever let anyone hurt you.*

Aloud, I say, "You must be insane, Sara. I will never, ever, ever get a Brazilian wax. Not ever. Not in a million years. Uh-uh. Not happening."

She stares at me, unconcerned.

"I already made the appointment. It's at 6:45. You're going to go. You'll love it. Shade will love it. It will release your inner lioness. Trust me."

"I'm not a lioness and I'm not going," I insist.

And in this moment, I mean it.

"Oh, you're going," she says as she takes her last bite of sandwich.

"Whatever you want to think," I shake my head as I gather my trash. "I've got to get back to work. Apparently, we're meeting our new Vice President today. I can't be late getting back."

Sara looks at me. "How's Brainy Brian doing? You know what they say about smart guys. They have big penises."

"No one says that," I sigh as I grab my purse. Brainy Brian is a recently divorced guy at work. He's decent looking, nice and makes good money. Sara has been convinced for several months now that I should date him, if only to practice. He's not my type—he's too wishy-washy. I need someone more assertive. And for some reason, I highly doubt that he has a big penis. Not that it matters.

Unless it is way too small.

But that doesn't matter to me anyway, because I'm not interested.

"And he's the same as always, Sara. Want me to get his number for you?"

"Maybe," she calls after me. "Call me tonight."

"Maybe," I call back.

I drive the short distance back to work from the little park that Sara and I always meet in to have lunch. I like the fountains there and she likes the shirtless male roller-bladers. It's also a perfect middle distance between her real estate office and my office building. We're all about compromise.

"Hello, Mrs. Lancaster," Larry, the front desk guy in the lobby greets me as I walk past.

"It's Ms. Lancaster now, Larry, "I remind him. He nods.

"I forgot. I'm sorry, Ms. Lancaster."

I smile and continue walking past. As I punch the elevator button, Taylor, my admin, rushes up to me as though she'd been waiting for me. She hands me messages, chattering a mile a minute as we wait for the elevator.

"Were you watching for me from the window?" I ask suspiciously.

"Of course not," she answers innocently. "I happened to be downstairs in the lounge at the vending machines."

"With my messages in your pocket?" I ask doubtfully. She shrugs.

"Coincidence?"

I have to smile. My assistant is a damn good one. She runs my calendar, she thinks for herself and she puts out fires for me all of the time. And even though she has a nose-ring, I'm happy to have her. One of my biggest dreads in life is the day she turns in her notice. She has assured me that this will never happen, that she will stay with me until we both die and then we'll be cremated and share the same mausoleum space. I suspect that she's being facetious.

"Oh," she says as she turns to me. "Rick the Dick's lawyer called. Said something about you running down his fiancée?"

(Side-note: Yes, I refer to my ex-husband as Rick the Dick to anyone who will listen, except for my daughter. It tends to stick with people. They re-use the term, which causes me great joy. Okay. Carry on.)

The elevator doors open and we step in. I sigh.

"Seriously? I can't believe he actually called his lawyer."

Taylor stares at me, waiting for an explanation.

"I might have slightly run over Vanessa at the mall yesterday morning. It wasn't a big thing and it was her fault. Please call back Rick's attorney and tell him to contact my lawyer, not me. I'm done talking to them."

"Done," she says, writing on her little notepad. "And you really ran her down? You're badass, boss."

I don't bother reminding her that it was an accident. I sort of like being called badass.

"Also, don't forget that we're meeting *your* new boss this afternoon," she reminds me as we wind our way through the marketing department that I oversee to get to my corner office. "You might not want to mention to him that you ran over someone yesterday."

I roll my eyes.

"I know," I tell her. "I haven't forgotten. Have you seen him yet?" I only ask this because Taylor keeps an eagle eye out for everything. Nothing escapes her attention. Plus, she networks with the other admins in the building. Nothing happens without them knowing about it.

"I have," she tells me proudly as I walk into my office and drop my briefcase into a chair at my conference table. "He's drop-dead gorgeous, for an older guy."

I eye her.

"What do you consider older?" Since Taylor is twenty-five, it's hard to say.

"Oh, I don't know," she muses she hands me an afternoon agenda. "Maybe thirty-five or forty."

"Hmm," I answer absently as I look at the agenda. It looks like my afternoon is shot because of the new guy. I have a meet-and-greet with him in his office at 3:00 after he addresses my department at 2:00. "Sounds promising."

"Definitely promising," Taylor confirms. "He's delicious."

I stop what I'm doing and look at her. "Don't even talk like that," I tell her. "It's against the rules to date co-workers."

"No, it's not," she answers. "It's just frowned upon. He could be the one for me. Do you really want to stand in the way of true love?"

I roll my eyes. Am I really surrounded by lunatics in every aspect of my life? Before I am able to answer, there is a soft rap at the door. Taylor and I both turn to find a middle-aged man striding confidently into my large office.

I inhale sharply, then hope that no one noticed.

He's a very, very attractive middle-aged man. Wow.

He's tall, maybe 6'1" or so. Dark hair that is cut close and clean. He's distinguished and sexy. And I'm once again reminded of how unfair Mother Nature actually is. And there's no way that she's a woman. A woman wouldn't give men such unfair advantages in life. She would make men the ones to give birth and get stretch-marks, then breastfeed until their male boobies drooped like two socks filled with wet sand. She would not allow them to age like this. No way.

Focus, Allison, I tell myself. *Focus on the beautiful man in front of you.*

Beautiful Man is wearing a dark, very expensive suit and he holds out his hand to shake mine.

"You must be Allison," he says. I find that I am staring so intensely into his dark blue eyes that I almost forget to answer. It takes Taylor nudging me to jolt me into action.

"Um, sorry. Yes, I'm Allison Lancaster. You can call me Alli."

"Good, "he says briskly, shaking my hand firmly. "I'm Alexander Harris. You can call me Alex. I've been looking forward to meeting you. I'm going to say a few words to your department here in a bit and then I look forward to speaking with you one-on-one. I'd like to hear how you do things, how things run, etc. Does that sound like a plan?"

He seems so familiar, like I've met him before. But I know that I haven't. I would definitely remember Beautiful Man. I mean, Alex. He's got a commanding presence about him. And he's gorgeous.

"Of course, "I tell him warmly. "I look forward to it."

"Alright, then," he says. His eyes crinkle a little at the corner when he smiles. I'm guessing he's either in his late thirties or early forties. And did I mention gorgeous? "I'll see you soon."

And he's gone.

Taylor turns to me.

"Did I tell you?" she sounds so knowing. So knowing that it is annoying.

"Well, I hope he has good things intended for this department," I say matter-of-factly. I drop into my chair and pick up my mouse, scrolling through my email. Taylor doesn't take the hint. She lingers, musing about Alex.

"Do you think he's married? I didn't see a ring on his finger."

"A lot of men don't wear rings," I tell her, not looking up. "Particularly the lying, cheating ones who don't want other women to know they're married. And you don't need to worry about his marital status, anyway. Just go and return my calls, please."

I smile to let her know that I'm not mad, but she knows that I mean it. I'm done pondering about the new guy.

Until twenty minutes later when I am standing in the back of the main conference room watching him speak to my employees.

He's at ease with them, laughing with them, talking frankly and openly about the changes he intends to make and the things he will keep the same. He easily commands the room, yet he doesn't act as though he is the new senior Vice President of Business Development. He acts like a friendly, knowledgeable neighbor who happens to be in the business.

As he speaks, his eyes find their way to mine. I can see warmth there, and a worldly wisdom and sparkling flecks of dark gray buried within the blue.

And once again, I have the feeling that I know him. It's frustrating.

He wraps things up and mingles for a bit, then makes his way to me.

"Would you be so kind as to meet me in my office in five minutes or so?" He smiles. And my knees feel weak.

Shit. This can't be good. I can't work with weak knees.

I nod. "Of course. I'll be there."

"Good." He smiles again and takes his leave. Taylor steps forward and nudges me.

"Can I say I told you so yet?"

I glare at her. "No. You can't."

"Okay," she chirps cheerfully. "It's enough to know that it's true."

She trots off to chatter with someone else, someone more willing to gush over our new boss with her. I do what any self-respecting and normal female does before meeting with her sexy-as-hell new boss. I sprint to the ladies room to freshen my lipstick.

Four point five minutes later, I am knocking softly on Alex's office door, my lips perfectly done.

"Come in," he calls from behind his desk. He stands up as I enter and waves his hand toward one of the two plush leather chairs in front of his large desk. "Please sit. Make yourself comfortable." I choose a seat.

"Thank you for chatting with me," Alex says cordially. I can't help but notice how he fills out his tailored shirt now that he's removed his suit jacket. I can practically see the muscles rippling behind the expensive cotton blend. This is a man who is no stranger to a gym.

"Of course," I answer demurely, or my best imitation of what I think demure ought to be. "I didn't know exactly what all you would want to discuss, so I'm afraid I'm a little unprepared. I didn't bring anything with me."

"Oh, you're fine," Alex says, smiling. "I simply wanted to get your take on this department and how things are currently run. You head it up, correct?"

I nod. "Yes. I've worked here for ten years. I started out as a middle manager and then after I earned my MBA, I started moving up the ranks."

Alex glances at a file on his desk. "And now you're an executive director in control of a very key department in this company. Marketing is imperative to any company's growth. You must feel the stress from time to time. Do you handle stress well?"

That's a very strange question, I decide as I stare at him.

"Yes, I do," I answer honestly.

"Good," he answers. "Because I see here that you're recently divorced. I don't usually pry into my staff's private affairs, but I'd like to know if you'll still be able to handle your professional stress level when it is combined with your personal stress?"

I stare at him and he stares back. He is calm and quiet and I am sure that he is unflappable. His dark gaze is unwavering. He is still beautiful, though, even when he is prying into my personal affairs and asking uncomfortable questions.

"My divorce was nine months ago," I tell him. "The bulk of the stress came during the first month. I'm fine now, I can assure you, just as I've been fine for the duration of my divorce. I've worked here for a long time. I know this company like the back of my hand. I can handle anything you throw at me and then ask for more."

My chin has automatically come up. It is annoying to me that this new guy thinks he can question my ability to do my job. I can do twice as much as he can with one hand tied behind my back. Of that, I am sure. He looks surprised by my determined tone.

"Allison, I meant no offense," he tells me soothingly. "I have been through a divorce. I only ask because I know what a toll it took on me. Those things are stressful. I just needed to know if I should let this department continue as it is for the time being or if you would be okay handling some of the changes that I would like to implement immediately. I wasn't questioning your abilities, I can assure you. I've heard glowing things about you from everyone here. You are well respected by your staff and your colleagues alike."

My dander immediately goes back down and my feathers become smooth again. If I had them, which of course I don't.

"Oh," I say. I don't really know what else *to* say. "I'm sorry if I sounded defensive. It's just that this company has been sort of a 'Good ol' boys' company for a long time. I had to claw my way to where I'm at. And I can't let it be thought that I am weak. Because I'm not."

"I have no doubt," Alex assures me. "And what do you mean by Good Ol' Boys?"

I flinch. "Um. Okay. Maybe that was a bad choice of words. What I meant was that there aren't a lot of women in executive positions here. It's mainly older men who have been here for a very long time. It's like a club. And I had to fight my way in."

"You had to kick down those glass ceilings with your high heels?" Alex grins and I inhale. Sweet Lord, the man's smile is breath-taking.

"In a matter of speaking," I nod.

He nods back. "Good. I like for my staff to have spunk. I like the fact that you've got it."

His gaze is appreciative and warm and that warmth transfers to me, flooding my face and my limbs. I have no idea how this is going to play out… me working for this new sexy boss. Particularly since he is as charming as he is handsome. That's a recipe for utter destruction if I've ever seen it.

"Can you tell me a little about how this department is run?" he asks. I am distracted by his hands. I have a thing for sexy male hands. If a man has long, strong fingers, I'm all in. And Alex certainly does. I grit my teeth.

"Of course," I answer.

So I spend the next thirty minutes ignoring his sexy hands and explaining how I have three directors, five senior managers and then forty lower level employees in this department who report to me and ultimately report to him. I explain the processes. I explain the current strategies that we're working on. I explain the company's current culture, even. And I do it all while ignoring his gorgeous hands.

I feel pretty proud of myself as I finish up.

I've obviously got amazing fortitude.

When I'm through speaking, I look at my new boss, waiting for a reaction. Alex sits back and swivels in his chair. His limbs are all sprawled out and he is very relaxed looking. And sexy. Did I mention sexy already?

He nods, thinking to himself. He spins and stares out the window. He temples his fingers, blowing on them. Finally, he turns back to me.

"I like it. I like the current hierarchy. We'll keep that in place. I have a special project that I'd like your input on, but we can discuss that later."

He stands up and holds out his hand.

"Allison, it has been a pleasure meeting you. I feel confident that you and I are going to work very well together. We'll make a great team."

I smile back and shake his hand, trying to ignore the electric sensations that ripple through my body as I touch him.

"It's a pleasure meeting you, too. I'm excited to see what ideas you have about moving the company forward."

He walks me to the door and I make my way back to my office.

As I walk in, I glance at the lavish furnishings, the leather chairs, the spacious area and the surrounding windows. I've worked hard as hell for this corner office. I'm not going to lose focus now over a new boss who just happens to be sexy and has a beautiful freaking smile.

I've got this.

I've *so* got this.

I continue feeling proud of myself all afternoon, as I stay in career-superwoman-mode instead of thinking about my new boss or even Shade. I do some sales trajectories, I work on a marketing plan and then I sit down with Taylor and go through my schedule for the following day. I do all of this without letting my mind wander.

I seriously am freaking Superwoman.

Not Superwoman enough, though, to cook dinner tonight. I'm too freaking tired for that nonsense. So on the way home, I stop and grab some take-out. Sophie will be happy about that, anyway. It will mean that we won't need to clean up the kitchen after dinner.

As I burst through the doors with food in one hand, my briefcase in the other and my bottle of water and mail balanced somewhere in between, I call out a hello.

No answer.

Okay. No big deal. I know she's home because she left the front door standing wide open when she came in from school and her backpack right inside the doorway. She probably just can't hear me because she's got her ear-buds in again. I might as well pay to have them surgically implanted in her head. It would make her life a lot easier, I'm sure.

I kick off my heels, sort through the mail and answer one quick e-mail on my phone before I hear laughter coming from the backyard through the French patio doors. And a male voice. My head snaps up. What the hell? Sophie knows the rules. No male friends over when I'm not home. I stomp to the patio, ready to ground her.

I throw open the doors and storm outside.

And stop dead in my tracks with my mouth hanging wide open.

Shade is in the pool with Sophie.

My daughter is with the gigolo that I had sex with.

Right now.

In my pool.

I am stunned. Appalled. Frozen in place.

He's not touching her. He's next to her in the water, motioning with his arms. He's obviously wearing swim-trunks. And he's obviously beautiful. And wet. And next to my freaking daughter.

Sophie looks up and sees me, waving.

"Hey, mom!" she calls, smiling.

Shade turns to greet me and his expression freezes.

He didn't know whose daughter he was with. That much is apparent.

But that doesn't change the fact that he is still here. With my daughter.

Did I mention *with my daughter??*

Obviously, I do the only thing that any healthy red-blooded female can do.

I freak out.

Big time.

Chapter Seven

(Or: I'm going to hell in a hand-basket)

"What the hell is going on?" I demand, practically breaking my neck to get to the water's edge. I reach in and haul Sophie out of the pool by her swimsuit straps, ignoring the fact that the chlorinated water is ruining my $250 silk blouse.

Sophie stares at me in shock, as does Shade.

And I have to admit. My high-pitched screech does sound a bit unbalanced.

But to be fair, I did just find my gigolo in my pool with my fifteen-year old daughter.

Have I mentioned that already?

"Mom," Sophie hisses. "Stop! You're embarrassing me!" This is whisper-yelled into my ear, as though Shade won't hear it when he is only three feet away. I glare down at her.

"Embarrassing *you*? You're in the pool, breaking my rules, with someone much older than you are!"

And someone who is much *younger* than me. But that little fact didn't stop me from screwing his brains out, now did it?

I ignore my inner voice because it is annoyingly correct.

Sophie stares at me silently. I raise an eyebrow as I feel my pulse beat in my temple.

"Well??"

"Um. Should I say something now?" Shade pipes up from behind Sophie.

He has emerged from the pool and I fight not to look at him. I'm sure he's devastatingly sexy in his wet swimtrunks. I don't need to see that right now. I need to stay pissed. And that's easy to do with Shade's next shocking words.

"Sophie told me that this was all approved by you. Her father has already paid in full, so everything is taken care of."

"Paid in full??? Her father paid you in full??"

I am screeching now, so loudly that my neighbors probably hear me. In fact, from the tone of my voice, they've probably inferred that I need 9-1-1 called because this is an emergency. And it is.

I calm myself just a bit, swallowing hard as I stare into Shade's deep blue, blue eyes.

"My ex-husband hired you for my daughter?"

Shade's cheek twitches a little and it appears that he fights back a grin. He towels off as he walks closer and I don't even glance at his practically naked body.

I really am Superwoman. And I have amazing fucking fortitude.

"Yes, he did," Shade confirms. "To be Sophie's swim coach. My name is Colby, Ms. Lancaster. I hope being here is alright."

"Swim coach," I repeat, feeling numb as realization slowly dawns on me. I had forgotten all about it.

"Yes, swim coach," Sophie snaps, her eyes spitting fire. "What is wrong with you? What did you think we were doing anyway?" She is glaring now and in this moment she looks so much like her father.

"I don't know," I say quietly. "It was just a surprise." I turn to Sophie. "I only just said yes the other day. How did you get it arranged so fast? And how did you talk your father into paying for it?"

Sophie looks smug. "He felt guilty. So you won't even have to worry about it. It's all taken care of."

I don't even bother asking how she managed it. Her father is much more inclined to want to write a check to get his fatherly obligations out of the way, rather than spend time with her. And I'm sure she knows it. And exploits it. Because that is what teenagers do. And in this case, I can't say I blame her. If anyone deserves to be exploited, it's Rick the Dick.

Shade/Colby looks at me and the laughter is gone from his eyes.

"Is it alright that I'm here?" he asks.

And I know what he really means.

Is it alright that my gigolo is here training my fifteen year old daughter in my pool when they are both barely covered in their swimsuits? Um, I don't know. How long do I have to ponder that? If I were a good mother, would it even be a question? I'd have already kicked him to the curb. Actually, I'd probably not know him in the first place because I wouldn't have hired him for sexual services. Right?

Ohmygod. I'm a horrible mother. I slept with a gigolo. And now he's in my pool. Child Protective Services are going to come and take me away because I have a gigolo in the pool with my underage daughter. I'm going to hell in a handbasket. I'm going to burn forever.

I'm on the verge of a breakdown.

And I think that Colby/Shade sees it, because he quickly turns to Sophie.

"You know what, Sophie? I'd like for you to do some laps for endurance. I want to see you swim twenty laps, then do ten of the drills that I showed you earlier. I should probably sit down with your mom and explain my training plans with her."

Sophie looks at me, waiting for my approval. I nod and she turns away, diving back into the glistening water. I stare down at her swimsuit clad form, wavering beneath the rippling turquoise water.

Shade/Colby takes my elbow and leads me into the kitchen. He pushes me gently into a chair in my kitchen and walks straight for my fridge. He pulls out a bottle of wine that I had re-corked last night and pours me a glass. He shoves it into my hands and sits down across from me.

"Are you okay?" he asks.

I gulp at my wine, draining it in three gigantic gulps.

"I don't know," I tell him honestly. "I let my friend talk me into seeing you the other night and now I find you in my pool training my daughter. I don't know if a good mother would let that happen."

"Why?" he asks in surprise. "Because of my other job? I can assure you of this: When I'm on Utopia's clock, I'm Shade. Any other time, including when I'm in the pool with your daughter, I'm Colby. And I'm very good at both of my jobs. I am completely professional. Your daughter will never see Shade. I'm not a pedophile, Alli."

I stare at him, at the way his brow is furrowed right now as he frowns at me. At the youthful tilt to his face. At the muscles that are still damp and are gleaming under the sun's rays which are pouring in through my kitchen windows. My heart pounds a little, remembering how those muscles had lifted me the other night and had bent me around until he was fucking me from behind.

I swallow hard.

"It's just strange. I was shocked. And now I don't know what to do."

Colby grins and with that ornery curve of his mouth, I see Shade come out.

"I told you before...I think you need for me to tell you what to do. You seemed to like it the other night. And I'm telling you right now. There is nothing inappropriate about me training your daughter. I'm an excellent swimmer. I swam four years at the college level and won several state championships. I know what I'm doing, I promise."

"Oh, I know you do," I say wryly. "I just... I don't know."

"I'll make you a deal," Colby/Shade says. "Give me five minutes of your time in here as Shade. Then come outside and watch the rest of my lesson with Sophie. If you don't see that I can totally and completely separate my two professions, I will gladly find you another swim coach for Sophie."

I look at him doubtfully. "You think you can convince me in five minutes?"

He looks smug. "I'm sure of it."

My chin lifts. "Fine. Challenge accepted."

Colby/Shade walks to the door and glances outside. "Okay. Sophie is still doing laps. Where is the closest room with a lock?"

I motion to the laundry room which is just off the kitchen. He drags me there and locks the door behind us.

"Five minutes," I remind him. He nods.

"Five minutes."

Without preamble, he quickly pulls down my skirt and stockings and lifts me onto the washer. He bends and with his cobalt blue eyes never leaving mine, his tongue fills me up. I gasp and arch against his mouth.

I'm self-conscious because I've been in stockings all day, because I haven't showered since this morning and because my daughter could walk into the house at any given time.

But the door is locked.

And this feels so freaking good.

"Relax," he says, his mouth hovering just above my skin. "You taste delicious."

He is a master with his tongue. And very, very good at his job.

I come in three minutes. I come quietly, without screaming, since I don't want Sophie to hear and come running. Shade watches my face as I come and I see satisfaction on his. When I am done convulsing (which takes approximately another thirty seconds), he slides me off the washer and against him.

His penis is hard and the velvety tip is pushed against me. I gulp.

He covers my mouth with his and I can taste myself there.

Holy cow. I'm such a freaking vixen, I think. *Or maybe I'm just a freak. Either way, there is freakiness involved.*

He pulls away. "Did you taste yourself?" I nod.

"You taste so fucking good," he tells me. "I'd like to fuck you now. But I won't. Because now, I'm going to be Colby and I'm going to go coach your daughter. But if you decide that you still require my services, you can call and make an appointment and I'll finish this. Alright?"

I nod. "Alright."

"Also, just so you know, you don't look nearly old enough to have a teenage daughter. You're gorgeous."

He pulls his swim trunks back on and he's gone before I know it.

I am utterly relaxed now, both by his compliment and his…um…services.

I lean against the dryer, trying to still my breathing for a second before I pull back on my skirt. I toss my stockings in the dirty clothes and smooth my hair down before I make my way out to the pool to watch the rest of Sophie's practice.

I recline on a pool lounger, soaking up the sun as I watch.

He was right. He's perfectly professional and he knows exactly what he's doing. And Rick has already paid for him. I have no good reason to say no.

At the end of the lesson, Sophie goes inside to get dressed and Colby comes and sits next to me. And it is clear that he is definitely Colby out here. Droplets from his wet hair drip onto my leg and I wipe them away.

"Well?" he grins. "What do you think?"

I shake my head.

"Fine. I can see that you are professional. And I have a horrible time saying no to Sophie. So, alright. You can continue."

Colby looks at me, his blue gaze glittering. He casually towels off his back. His wide, strong, sexy back. I restrain myself from watching. I seriously continue to amaze myself with my fortitude.

"I can continue as Sophie's coach? Or I can continue as Shade... for you?"

He watches me, waiting for my answer.

I glance at his rippling chest, as his bulging tanned biceps, at the dimple in his left cheek. And then I remember his erect penis pressed against me in the laundry room and sigh.

"Both."

He grins because he knows that he has won.

And I program his cell number into my own phone that evening.

I'm probably going to burn in hell for all of eternity. But when I do, at least it will have been worth it.

Chapter Eight

(Or: To Hair or Not to Hair? It's not even a sane question)

"You've got to be freaking kidding me," Sara exclaims, staring at me from across the table. We're at lunch again, at our usual table in the park between our office buildings. "And you didn't think this was important enough to call me about last night? What is wrong with you? This breaks like every rule in the BFF handbook!"

"I know," I sigh, picking at my turkey on whole wheat. "I just felt exhausted. I didn't even want to re-hash it. It makes me feel like a horrible mother. First I had sex with a gigolo. Then the gigolo ends up in my pool with my daughter. Then said gigolo performs oral sex on me while my daughter swims laps, then I agree to let previously mentioned gigolo continue training my daughter while I continue using his sexual services. Am I insane?"

Sara nods.

"Yes. But in a good way," she rushes to reassure me. "You've been too uptight for too many years. You saw for yourself- Colby can be Colby with Sophie and he can be Shade with you. Trust me. As Sophie's godmother, I would never steer you wrong on this topic. I love that girl. And not even one fine looking piece of dick will sway me from doing what's right where she's concerned. In my opinion, you're just fine. Keep an eye on it. And if anything seems inappropriate, fire his amazingly sexy ass. Until then, enjoy him. Enjoy the scenery when he's in your pool. Then bang his brains out when you see him on the weekends. That's my final answer."

She folds her arms over her chest as though she is the Great and Powerful Oz, and the Great and Powerful Oz has spoken. I roll my eyes.

"Well, I'm glad that's cleared up," I say wryly as I reach for my lemonade. I find myself wishing that it contained vodka. Sara glares at me.

"I'm serious," she says. "You're fine. Now, changing the subject… I need you to date Brian."

I almost break my neck as I gape at her.

"Have you lost your mind?" I ask. "He's as boring as a plain white button-up. I can't date him. I'd want to slit my wrists within the first thirty minutes. No lie, Sara."

She sighs, as though I have tried her patience for the last time.

"First, it would depend on who is wearing the white button up as to how boring it is. And second, Brainy Brian will be great practice for you in the dating world. I need for you to get your date on. And I need for you to do it well. I am not having you moping around anymore, staying home on weekends alone when Sophie is at her dad's. More importantly, I can't be babysitting you every weekend. There are places for me to go and people to do."

I stare at my best friend, wondering if aliens have taken over her body.

"Do you even know me at all? Wasn't it me who went to Utopia with you last weekend? And Sophie is hardly ever at her dad's. And you don't babysit me! Do you? What is with you?"

Sara shrugs as she takes an elegant bite of her bean sprout wrap.

"I just feel a certain responsibility to get you back out on the market. My experiment with Shade went so much better than expected. And speaking of, since you are keeping Shade's…services, it's going to work out very well now that you're dating."

"I'm not dating!" I practically shout at her. The couple at the nearest table look over at me, startled. I settle myself down. "Not yet, anyway. Do you even listen to me?"

Sara levels a stare at me, unflustered.

"Not usually. Anyway. As I was saying, you'll be able to date without the added pressure of whether or not to have sex with your date now. Isn't that perfect? You can polish your dating skills without having to worry about the question of 'will you or won't you sleep with the guy at the end of the night'? You can take out your sexual frustrations on Shade, because you're paying him to sleep with you. It's a perfect arrangement. And I think you should begin your dating life with Brainy Brian. Because he's easy and safe and won't break your heart."

I seriously want to pull my hair out. Or her hair out. Except hers is too short to really get a good grip on. We're back to my hair. I sigh.

"Sara, I work with Brian. I don't think it's a good idea to date someone who I work with. Especially when I know that I'm not interested in him for the long term."

"Good Lord, Alli!" she snaps. She's quickly losing patience with my arguments, I can tell. "Don't you get it? You're not going to settle down with anyone else for a very long time. We got that out of our system with Rick, didn't we? You're going to have fun. But in order to do that, you have to learn how to interact with the opposite sex. You've forgotten how to flirt, my sweet."

I rub the middle part of my forehead because it is rapidly growing a headache.

As I do, my phone buzzes. I look down and find a text from Shade. My eyes widen and I snatch up my phone to read it.

Do you want me yet?

I must look dumbfounded because Sara starts questioning me.

"What? Who is it? What's wrong?"

I shake my head, laying my phone back down in my lap.

"Nothing's wrong. Shade just texted me. I wasn't expecting this kind of interaction with him. That's all."

Sara wrinkles her forehead. "A text? Really? That's sort of strange. Chaz doesn't text me except to confirm dates and times and whatnot."

I'm puzzled. "Maybe he's just flirting with me to make sure that he keeps me as a customer," I speculate. "That's probably it, actually. It's good for business, right? He wants to keep me interested. It's good sales strategy."

"I don't know," Sara muses. "Life does not consist of sales strategy alone. But you might be right. Who knows?"

"Yep. Who knows," I repeat.

I text him back.

Of course.

Because it's true. I do want him. I'm a wanton, wanton, middle-aged sex fiend. Does that make me a cougar?

I turn to Sara. "Does this make me a cougar?"

She laughs a maniacal laugh, one that makes me instantly afraid. I look at her.

"Well, am I?"

"Oh, my dear little Alli. I think the common definition of a cougar is an older woman who seeks out younger men. I think. And I don't know if you are old enough to technically be considered a cougar. But, in my opinion, a cougar is a sexual woman who is comfortable in her skin and knows what she wants. And if she doesn't know what she wants, then like you, she is working hard on figuring it out. She's sexy and she's confident and sometimes, she might happen to have sex with a younger man. Because she's confident and anything goes. That's what I view a cougar to be. And so yes, I think you might be one."

I gulp. Both at the name and at her definition.

"Okay," I nod. "I'm a cougar. That's alright. I'm okay."

"Are you?" Sara asks, the barest hint of concern on her perfectly made-up face. "Are you trying to convince me or you?"

"Um, me, obviously," I snort. "But it's fine. I'm fine. I'm a cougar and I'm fine."

Sara shakes her head. "You're saying *fine* too many times. It's a sign of insanity. Oh- I forgot. Be ready for our appointment to get waxed tomorrow evening. 6:45. I'll pick you up. Don't wear jeans—wear something loose. Like a skirt. Trust me, you won't want any pressure on your cootch afterward."

I roll my eyes. "Cootch? Seriously? Could you think of a more disgusting word?"

"Probably, if you give me a minute," Sara answers, picking up her trash. "Just be ready when I pick you up."

She stands up.

"I'm not getting a Brazilian," I insist.

"Yes, you are," she insists back. "You're going to love it. You're a strong, independent cougar. And as such, you need a Brazilian. All sexy cougars have Brazilians. Have I steered you wrong yet?"

"How about that time that…" I pause, trying to think of something. "Okay, how about that time when…" I pause again. "Okay, fine. I've got nothing right this second. But there have been times. I know it."

Sara grins beatifically at me.

"Perhaps. But those times aren't right now. You're going to be smooth and silky as a baby's bum. You're going to love it. And Shade's gonna love it. I'll pick you up at 6:45. Oh, and you might want to take two ibuprofen ahead of time."

"What?" I yelp.

But she's already walking away in her strikingly gorgeous Jimmy Choos, swishing her hips so emphatically that every man in the near vicinity is gazing at her ass. And since I personally hate to disrupt a good exit, I let her go.

I'll think on the Brazilian.

Unfortunately, I get side-tracked by work and life, and I forget to think about it. And I forget to do research on it.

It isn't until 6:45 the following night when I am clearing away the dinner dishes and I hear a car in my drive that I remember.

And I curse loudly enough to make any sailor or truck-driver proud.

"What?" Sophie looks up from where she has settled in to do homework as she eats a brownie. I shake my head.

"Nothing, sweets. I just forgot that I promised Aunt Sara that I would help her this evening."

"With what?" Sophie asks curiously. I draw a blank.

"Um, nothing," I stutter.

And I am saved by Sara's red head poking into my kitchen.

"Are you ready?" she calls. "And I don't want to hear any arguments. Oh, hi, Soph," she coos to my daughter.

"What are you two up to?" Sophie asks suspiciously, narrowing her hazel eyes.

"Us?" Sara splays a manicured hand across her bosom, which is perfectly displayed in a low-cut, tight blouse. I've got to hand it to her. Sara is truly playing up this cougar thing.

"We're doing nothing. Your mom simply needs my help tonight."

Sophie's eyes instantly grow narrower. "Mom said she was helping *you*."

"Oh, that's right," Sara gushes. "She's helping me. With something."

Sophie rolls her eyes. "You guys are weird. I've got homework to do anyway." She picks up her books and trudges down the hall toward her bedroom.

"I won't be late!" I call after her. She waves at me over her shoulder without saying anything.

I turn to Sara with a sigh. "Alright, fine. I'll do it."

She looks at me innocently. "Was it ever a question?"

I sigh again. I am clearly surrounded by lunatics.

****

Twenty minutes later, I am terrified.

I am naked from the waist down, flat on my back with a tiny towel covering up my female parts. A tiny little chick with an eyebrow ring is getting the wax ready and I'm panting again. Did I mention that the wax will be hot? And that it is going on my private, tender female parts? I pant harder.

"Calm down," Sara instructs, sitting next to me.

They don't usually allow spectators in, but Sara convinced them that I would need my hand held. At the moment, I think I would rather hold hands with the devil himself, considering how it is Sara's fault that I am in this predicament in the first place.

"Your vagina will thank you," she announces to me. "So suck it up and put your big girl panties on. You're going to be fine."

"I can't put my big girl panties on," I hiss. "Because I'm getting the hair on my vagina ripped out by the roots. So, obviously, I can't pull up any panties, big-girl or otherwise."

Sara rolls her eyes.

"Why do you have to be so melodramatic?" she asks, peering at me over the top of her fashion magazine. "This is for your own good. Do you really want to walk around with something that needs a weed-wacker?"

The Waxer-Girl (because I have no idea what her true title is) giggles as she turns around, a wooden spatula thingie in her hand. I gulp and I know my eyes are wild as I assess the room for an escape hatch. Without even looking up, Sara puts a hand on my arm.

"Don't even think about it," she says, while still reading her article.

"I'm going to throw up," I try.

"No, you're not," she answers.

"I have cramps," I attempt.

"Doesn't matter," she replies.

"I think I'm pregnant," I hedge, as a last attempt.

"Impossible," she says heartlessly. "And irrelevant. Preggos need bald vajayjays too. Now, let's get on with it, shall we?"

She's looking at me now, with one thinly sculpted brow practically raised into her red hairline. I gulp and nod, squeezing my eyes shut. I do not want to watch this. At all.

"For the record," I tell Sara while keeping my eyes tightly closed, "I do not need a weed-wacker."

"Irrelevant," she says again, her attention once again absorbed by her magazine.

I sigh.

Waxer-Girl clatters around a little bit by my elbow and then examines my vag.

"Okay, Ms. Lancaster," she says. "I'm just going to first spread the wax, then…"

I interrupt her. "I don't want to know," I say firmly. "Just do it. I'm not looking."

"Okay, m'am," she says. I can tell she's smiling, but I don't care. Considering the circumstances, I also overlook the fact that she called me the dreaded *m'am*.

I feel the wax, hotter than I would have imagined, getting spread on the part of me that should never be exposed in a salon or anywhere else with fluorescent lighting. Ever. Except in a doctor's office which can't be helped.

She puts something thin on top of the wax. Then she pats it down. And pats some more. And since I have had my eyebrows waxed faithfully every six weeks like clockwork since I was a teenager, I know what comes next. I brace for it. And brace for it. And hold my breath and brace for it again.

And then it comes.

Riiiiiiipppppppppp.

The room literally blurs for a second. I think I might actually be having an aneurysm from the white-hot pain. I can barely even see straight.

"Holy shit!" I yelp. I grab ahold of Sara's arm now and sink my fingernails into it.

"Oh, so now you want to hold my hand?" Sara says with interest. And a little bit of snark.

"No," I snarl. "Now I would like to rip your hand off. Just like you just had my pubic hairs ripped off. It's only fitting, don't you think?"

She shakes her head. "Oh, Alli. You truly are a drama queen. Now I know where Sophie gets it. You're going to survive, trust me."

"I might," I tell her confidently. "But I doubt *you* will."

Sara rolls her eyes as the second round of wax gets applied.

Pat, pat, pat.

I cringe, getting ready.

Riiiiiipppppppp.

I yelp again. And dig my nails deeper into Sara's arm. If possible, that was worse than the first time.

"Oh, holy pygmy monkeys," I moan, wanting desperately to cradle my vagina and sing to it.

I'm sorry, my pet, I tell it silently. *I know I promised that I wouldn't hurt you. It was her idea. Not mine.*

"Alli, you're going to be fine," Sara says impatiently. "Beauty comes with a price." I can hear a tiny bit of sympathy in her voice now, though. Because of that, I wonder if I'm bleeding down there.

"Not now, Sara," I say through gritted teeth. "I'm apologizing to my vagina."

Waxer-Girl laughs aloud now, and I glare at her. She averts her gaze instantly and applies more wax.

Holy Sheep Shit.

"How many rounds of wax does this usually take?" I manage to ask finally.

Pat, pat, pat.

Riiiiiipppppppp.

I'm literally sweating now. I think I'm pale too, like all of the color has leached out of my skin. This waxer girl from hell has taken my pigment along with my pubes, apparently.

"I don't know," Waxer Girl From Hell answers cheerfully. "Several."

Seven rounds later, I am drenched through to the bone. Sweat pours off my forehead and I think I am shaking uncontrollably. I'm also weeping in my head.

Waxer-Girl finally tells me, "Okay, that should do it. Now I need you to turn over."

I twist around and look at her. Turn over??

"And spread your butt cheeks."

I think I faint.

I do.

I definitely faint.

Because when I wake up, I have been turned over onto my stomach and Sara is holding my butt cheeks open.

"What the hell?" I screech, trying to get up.

"Do it!" Sara yells to Waxer-Girl. "Hurry up!"

Riiiiiiipppppppp.

I might never walk again.

Chapter Nine

(Or: There is a reason why God created razors)

"I can't believe you did this to me," I moan as I hobble out to Sara's car. Thank god she told me not to wear jeans. I wouldn't be able to tolerate anything rubbing against my girl right now. And by girl, I of course mean my vagina.

Sara, Miss Masochism herself, is marching briskly along like she didn't just have her pubic hairs all yanked out.

"I also can't believe that it didn't hurt you like it hurt me and that you also held my butt cheeks apart with your bare hands. What is wrong with you??"

I try to glare at her but am interrupted by the shooting pains originating from my vaginal region when I try to sit in Sara's car.

"Owwwwww!" I howl. "Holy shit, I think I'm going to die. How am I going to sit in my office chair tomorrow?"

I curl carefully onto my side, balancing precariously on one butt cheek, trying to avoid any and all pressure on my private parts.

Sara glances at me. "It doesn't hurt nearly so much after the first time," she tells me. "And I held your butt cheeks apart because I thought it would be best to have her finish while you were out."

"Yes!" I hiss. "I passed out. Shouldn't that have told you something? Like it hurt too effing much to continue, maybe? Owwwww!" I howl again.

By this time, passersby are staring at us in concern. I roll my window up.

Sara turns up the radio so she doesn't have to hear me complain.

And then I give up and internally sob for the rest of the drive to my house instead.

"See you at lunch?" Sara asks cheerfully as I crawl carefully out of her car and into my driveway.

I growl in response and she drives away.

I hobble into my house, digging for a bag of frozen peas and collapse onto a loveseat in the living room with the bag firmly planted between my legs.

Since every light in the house is off, I am guessing that Sophie has gone down the street to her best friend Hayley's house. I am safe lying here like this for a while.

I close my eyes.

And I must drift off because I am awakened by a male voice.

"Alli, are you alright?"

My eyes fly open to find Shade standing above me.

I am confused.

"Am I dreaming?" I ask groggily. He smiles, like an angel or something equally as beautiful.

"No. I texted you. I left my watch by your pool- I just realized it today. I texted you a few times and you didn't answer, so I texted Sophie and asked if I could stop by and get it. I hope that's okay. I saw you from the window so I just walked in your door. It was open."

What the hell? People can see me lying here with peas on my crotch from the window??

I look in that direction in alarm and quickly sit up, wincing in pain as I do.

"What's wrong?" Shade asks in concern, bending down to examine me.

"Don't," I push him away self-consciously. "It's nothing."

My cheeks flush and I am dying of embarrassment. Beautiful, perfect Shade doesn't need to know what I just did to my vagina.

"You had a Brazilian, didn't you?" he asks knowingly, as he straightens back up.

Correction. I only thought I wanted to die before. In actuality, I want to die *now.*

I nod pitifully.

He shakes his head and scoops me up, carrying me easily.

"Which way to your bedroom?" he asks. I point and he carries.

"Do you have aloe?" he asks, sitting me carefully on my bed.

I nod. "In the hall closet."

He leaves to get it and closes my bedroom door behind him when he returns.

"In case Sophie comes home," he explains.

Good idea.

He approaches me again and bends, wriggling my skirt up gently. With the most feather-light of touches, he applies the aloe. And I do feel better.

He straightens.

"Do you have any tea bags?"

I stare at him. What kind of question is that?

"In the kitchen," I answer uncertainly.

He ducks out. And then returns a few minutes later with some soaking wet teabags on a saucer. I eye him with a raised and suspicious eyebrow.

"Trust me," he says. "This will make you feel better. We just have to let them cool for a bit."

He sets the saucer next to me and then examines my poor, bald vag area. And I do have to admit that it looks amazing, even though it feels like freaking hell.

"It would be a good idea to get some tea-tree oil tomorrow," he tells me, as he sits down next to me "It prevents any ingrown hairs. Whatever possessed you to get this done?"

He's curious now and watching me. He's also picked up my hand and is stroking my thumb. I force my heart beat to slow. Obviously, he's used to touching people, considering his profession. This doesn't mean anything special. He's just being sweet.

"I don't know," I mumble. "Well, actually I do. Sara talked me into it."

He nods. "Red-headed friend from the other night?"

I nod.

"Figures," he mutters. Then he looks at me again. "You don't need to do shit like this, Allison. You're beautiful the way you are. God invented razors for a reason- to use. You don't need to get waxed."

I smile for the first time this evening.

"I might love you now," I announce. And he grins.

"Don't get too attached," he kids. "I never fall in love with clients."

And even though he was joking, his words hit home with me. I'm a client. I pay him to be nice to me. What the hell am I doing?

Shade looks at my expression. "I was just kidding!" he says quickly. "I mean, I don't date clients on a personal basis...but..."

"It's okay," I tell him. "You don't have to explain. How did you get started in this job, anyway?"

He settles back on my cushions and stares at the ceiling, biting his lip for a second as he thinks.

"I don't know. I had a friend who talked me into it. I'm a guy, and of course, I like to have sex. It seemed like a good idea. My dad wanted me to go into the business field and I don't think that's for me. But I don't know what I want to do yet."

I think about that.

"Did you go to college?"

"Yep. I graduated with a degree in Sociology. I don't know that I want to go to graduate school, but my father is convinced that I need an MBA."

I stare down at his leg, which is pressed against mine. His is strong and long.

"You don't need an MBA if you don't want to go into business," I tell him. "But it wouldn't hurt to have in case you do eventually decide to go down that road. You're still young. You'll figure it out."

"I know," he tells me, turning onto his side and pushing a stray lock of my hair behind my ear. "I have confidence in that. My father is the one who doesn't."

"Oh, he'll come around," I say absently as I look down at Shade's gorgeous body. I still can't quite believe I have a sexy guy like him on my bed right now and I am completely out of commission. I curse every sex god that there is.

Shade sits up and pokes at the tea bags. "These are cool enough now. Hold still."

He arranges the wet, clumpy bags on my bald, bald vagina.

"Let these sit for a while," he instructs. "Something about them soothes the skin. I can't remember why. But I do know that it works."

"Okay," I answer, because honestly, it feels better already. "This is a whole new definition of tea-bagging, you know."

He laughs, true amusement passing over his face which causes his gorgeous eyes to sparkle. It reminds me of how young he is.

"I should go before Sophie comes home," he says. "Thank you for letting me get my watch."

"Thank you for rubbing aloe onto my vagina," I answer.

He grins. "Surprisingly, that's something I don't hear every day."

I laugh and my phone rings.

I start to reach for it and wince.

Shade shakes his head and retrieves it, handing it to me.

"Hello?" I answer. Shade motions toward the bathroom. I shake my head. Of course he can use it. His penis has been inside of my body. It isn't a problem for it to be inside of my bathroom, too.

"Allison? It's Brian. From work."

I freeze.

Oh God. Not right now. Really?? Right now, when I am lying with my female business exposed and rubbed with aloe and covered in wet tea bags, and while my gigolo is within hearing distance? What kind of sick joke is Fate trying to play on me? But of course I don't say that.

"Hi Brian," I say instead.

"Hey, I hope this isn't a bad time. But I was thinking about you today. And I know it's hard after a divorce to get back out there. And I've been through that. So I just thought I'd ask you to dinner. If you'd like."

Long pause.

There is no way that this is coincidental. But the question is, how did Sara get to him? This is her handiwork. I can feel it.

But worse, I can feel Brian's nervousness. He is nervous about calling me and I find that I can't bring myself to reject him. Even though Shade has emerged from the bathroom now and is leaning against the doorway watching me with interest.

"Oh. Um. Yes. I'd love to. Just a friendly dinner? That would be fun."

That was me, subtly pointing out that we would be going out as friends.

I hope he gets the point.

"Absolutely," he answers, obviously relieved. "Just a friendly dinner. Friday night?"

"Sure," I answer.

"Great. We can settle the details later. Have a great night, Allison."

"You too, Brian."

We hang up and I want to throw my phone.

"Freaking Sara!" I grouse. Shade looks even more interested, so I explain. And he's amused. I'm not so much.

"This could be fun," he assures me. "Trust me. Weren't you going to make an appointment with me on Friday night?"

I look at him, not seeing his point.

"Yes. But I still can... I'll just go to dinner first."

Shade nods, a mischievous light in his blue, blue eyes.

"You sure will," he says and I am instantly nervous.

"What are you thinking?" I ask. If I weren't in so much pain still, I would back away slowly.

"I'm going to send you something," he tells me. "It will be fun. I want you to wear it when you go out on your date with Brian—before you come see me. Do you promise?"

I stare at him. "I don't know. Do you promise that I'll like it? And that it will fit?"

He nods, his eyes sparkling.

"Oh, I promise...both that you will love it and that it will fit."

"Hmm. Okay. I can't say no to that, then."

He smiles, satisfied.

"Perfect. I'll see you Friday. Dream about me."

"Okay." I grin at his cockiness.

He leaves and I close my eyes.

Lo and behold, later that night when I finally go to sleep after Sophie returns home, I do dream about him.

And they aren't PG-13 dreams, either.

****

My vagina has decided that she hates me.

This much is true and apparent.

I wake up with my crotch still on fire. Sort of. It's okay, really, until it rubs against something. Like fabric or a chair or a sheet or anything at all. It's a little inconvenient since I can't go to work naked.

I groan as I step into the shower, imagining the day I'm going to have.

And then I scream as the hot water runs down over my vag. It may as well be boiling.

Cold water!

Cold water!

Cold water!

My brain is screaming at me and I fumble with the water, turning it all the way over to cold. Which of course leaves me screaming and hopping as I try to adjust it to a tepid temperature that I can actually stand in while I wash my hair.

All the commotion, of course, brings Sophie running into my bathroom.

"Are you alright?" she shouts. "Did you fall?"

"I'm fine!" I call back. "Just had a surge of hot water scald me to death. It's fine. Go get ready for school. But hey- can you put the tea kettle on the stove on your way back through the kitchen?"

"Okay," she answers, already turning around. Her concern for my well-being is overwhelming. I could have first degree burns in here and she wouldn't care.

I'm going to be a bitch today. I can already tell. It's just one of those days.

I take the shortest shower in the history of mankind, then towel off before I pad to the kitchen and make a cup of tea with six teabags. I dunk them a few times, then lay them on a saucer to cool, just as I watched Shade do it last night.

I return to my room and pull on a black pencil skirt, and a hot pink silk blouse. I have the perfect pair of heels to match it. By this time, my tea bags have cooled enough, so I shove my skirt up to my waist, lay flat on my back on my bed and cover my crotch with the wet bags.

Ahhhhhhh. If my vagina had a nirvana, this might be it. Well, this would be its Nirvana today, anyway. My vagina is sort of a fickle little thing.

I am remembering how Shade carefully arranged the bags for me last night, his long fingers moving them around just so, when I hear a rushed voice.

"Hey, mom, I need some money for lunch---"

Sophie bursts into my room and skids to a stop, her look a priceless cross between horror and shock. I'm sure it mirrors my own. I scramble to sit up and yank my skirt down, and as I do, the wet tea bags scatter on the white carpet of my bedroom.

I'm not sure what to do first, pick them up before they stain or try to explain to my daughter what she just saw.

"Um." I bend to yank the bags up and Sophie shakes her head.

"You are so weird, mom."

And she walks back out.

"There's money in my wallet!" I call to her.

No answer.

I've probably scarred my kid for life.

I grab my cell phone and text Sara.

I so hate you right now.

I jog down the hall and get a sponge, then clean up the tea spots on my carpet. Because of this whole debacle, which has all stemmed from Sara, I only have a few minutes to throw some makeup on and yank a brush through my hair. I have a meeting first thing this morning and I can't be late because I'm pretty sure Alex will be sitting in.

I decide against wearing stockings or even panties today. I can't believe I'm doing this, but I can't have anything touching my girl. I just can't. If I weren't in so much pain, I would feel naughty for going to work sans panties.

As it is, I just feel grumpy. When I get in my car, I carefully arrange Brazilian Baldy so that she's not rubbing against my seat. My phone buzzes. It's Sara.

That was your vagina talking, not you. You love me. You have to. Because I know all of your secrets.

I sigh. She has a point.

Fine. My vagina hates you, I answer.

I don't even have time to stop and get coffee on the way to work, which definitely doesn't bode well for my day.

As I breeze past Taylor, I growl, "I need coffee."

She takes one look at my face and scrambles to her feet, presumably to find me some. I love that girl. She knows me so well. And also, she doesn't want to put up with me sans caffeine. I know that much is true because *I* don't want to put up with me sans caffeine either.

"Alli," she calls from behind me, but I ignore her. I'm so not in the mood for anything right now until I have imbibed at least two cups.

"I'm not in the mood yet," I call back as I open my office door.

I'm not usually such a bitch, but a raw crotch will do that to a person.

I stalk into my office and stop.

Alex is sitting casually on the couch, his legs propped up while he reads the Wall Street Journal. I stare. He glances up. He's got two cups from a local coffee house sitting next to him. He is wearing black pinstripe slacks and a white button-up. He looks fresh and handsome and it's apparent that *he* is certainly not suffering from a raw crotch.

And holy shit. Sara was right. It definitely depends on who is wearing the button-up as to how boring it is.

This white-button up is not boring at all. When it is stretched across two strong shoulders like that, how *could* it be boring?

Alex smiles.

It's a beautiful smile that makes the corners of his gorgeous eyes crinkle.

"I took a chance and guessed that you like Kona coffee," he says cheerfully, handing me one of the cups. "Sugar and cream. I'm sorry if it's not right."

"Bless you," I say as I grab the cup greedily from his fingers. I restrain myself from gulping it down in two swallows. Instead, I sip it like a lady. A lady who has been wandering in the desert for two weeks and is ready to die from thirst, that is.

Alex laughs.

"Bad morning?"

I lower the cup. If I admit it, he might think I can't handle personal stress after all. And I can't tell him about my vag problems.

"Um. Just busy already," I tell him.

"Well, I won't keep you. I just wanted to tell you that I'll be sitting in your staff meeting today. I just want to get a feel for your department. No big thing. I just didn't want you to feel surprised."

I smile. I'm feeling gracious now that the caffeine is circulating through my veins.

"It's fine. I expected that you would join us today and obviously, you are welcome any time. Is there anything in particular you want us to cover?"

Alex shakes his sexy head.

"No. Just go on with business as usual. If I have questions, I'll ask."

He picks up his paper and takes his leave. He is barely gone before I buzz for Taylor. She walks in and I smile pleasantly.

"Is there any reason why you didn't mention as I walked past you that our new boss was waiting for me in my office?"

She smiles back like the saucy wench that she is.

"Yes. You said that you weren't in the mood for it yet."

I take four deep breaths and mentally pick up my stapler and throw it at her smiling head. She smiles wider, as if she knows my thoughts.

"In the future," I say calmly, still smiling, "Please let me know when Alex Harris is waiting for me, even if I say that I'm not in the mood to hear it."

She nods cheerfully. "Will do, boss. Should I also always tell you if you have lipstick on your teeth?"

I nod back. "Of course."

She smiles. "You do."

"Son of a bitch!" I snap, as I remember how I had smiled widely at Alex. I rub furiously at my teeth with my finger as a toothbrush. Why, oh why, did I have to wear hot pink lipstick today of all freaking days?

I bare my teeth to her like a horse.

"Is it gone?"

She is nodding exactly at the same time as Alex walks back into my office. He stops short and stares at my horse-mouth, then laughs.

"Oh, good. I see your assistant told you about the lipstick. I wasn't sure if I should or..." he trails off and I wish that I could melt into the floor.

Taylor slips back out, her skinny shoulders shaking, and I can hear her laughing at her desk. I make a mental note to kill her later. Right after I staple her fingertips to her desk.

I look at Alex. "I'm sorry. It's been an unusually hectic morning. I forgot to check my lipstick in the car. And yes. To answer your question, any woman would be grateful if you told her that she had lipstick on her teeth. Or about anything else that she has forgotten to check."

He nods and smiles. "Noted, then. From now on, if I notice something like that, I'll tell you. I just never know what will offend someone."

He's such a warm person. It's a little surprising since he holds such an important position. But I can tell that he likes to joke and laugh. And I love that kind of person. So combine that with his devastating good looks and I might be in serious trouble here.

"Oh, I don't offend easily," I promise him. "Seriously, you can treat me like one of the guys. Just pretend that I don't have ovaries."

He raises an eyebrow. "Um, okay. I'll try that. What I was coming back for, though, was to see if you had a file on our new client, Malochec? I'd like to look through it."

"Of course," I tell him. I buzz Taylor and asked her to bring it in. She trots in a couple of minutes later and hands it to me and I pass it to Alex. Our fingers touch and I feel a jolt of imaginary electricity. He looks at me, seemingly oblivious.

"Perfect," he says. "I'll see you in a few."

I gather a few things and then follow him out, making my way to the conference room. I am painfully aware of my raw crotch. Unfortunately, the tea bags' effect doesn't last that long. If I could limp without drawing attention to myself, I so would.

As it is, I walk stiffly in and take my normal seat.

Alex sits across from me and I grab a pen to make notes. I start the meeting as I usually do and allow the various managers to speak to their various points, current projects and so on. I squirm uncomfortably in my seat for the duration, spreading my knees slightly to allow the cool air to brush over my girl.

I listen to Jack, Herb, Angela and Marla all speak. I ask if there are any concerns that I need to know about. I silently pray that there isn't. Everyone shakes their heads. Like me, they just want to go about their business and end this meeting. Not for the same reason, though, I'm sure. So, I smile and turn to Alex.

"Would you like to end the meeting?"

And I'm surprised when I am speaking to his hunched back because he's digging under the table. I pause and he comes back up with a pen in his hand, his cheeks slightly flushed, probably from being upside down.

"What?" he asks, seemingly flustered.

"I said, would you like to end the meeting?" I repeat politely.

"Oh. Um, no. I have a couple of questions for Herb and Angela, but I'll come by your offices later in the day. Everyone have a good Thursday!"

Everyone grabs their coffee and their notebooks and makes a mad dash for the door. Except for Alex. He stays put and after everyone else has left, he turns to me. I don't know what to make of his expression. It's sort of amused, sort of confused, sort of shocked. I'm intrigued as I wait for him to speak.

"Remember when you said that if you ever forget something again, not to hesitate to tell you, because you wouldn't get offended?"

I nod, confused. "Yes, since it was just this morning, I do remember that."

He smiles. "Great. Because you seem to have forgotten your underwear today and I thought you might want to know."

He picks up his coffee and strolls out of the conference room.

And I seriously want to effing die.

Chapter Ten

(Or: Embarrassment is a wine best served cold)

I storm as quickly as I can back to my office and pick up my phone. I type so fast and furious that it actually hurts my texting finger.

You. Me. Wine. My patio. Tonight.

I send this to Sara.

And then I add, *You're lucky that I haven't hired a hit man.*

I stay in my office as much as I can all day for two reasons.

1) Because my crotch hurts too much to walk; and
2) Because I will die if I have to look Alex in the eye right now.

I try to decide how best to handle this. I can't believe he saw my dainty lady bits from under the table and I am absolutely mortified. Alex is going to think that I'm a flipping freak. And I can't believe that he even said anything! But to be fair, I did tell him that I never get offended. And that's partially true.

I'm not offended.

I'm humiliated. And there is a difference.

Good Lord.

I re-position myself in my seat trying to stay off of said dainty lady bits. I do a quick search online to see when I can expect the pain to subside. Most articles say that the pain should've decreased after the first night.

Wrong.

I cringe as I move.

This is horrible.

Absolutely freaking horrible. And it is the last time I listen to Sara. Ever.

My pity-party is interrupted by Taylor knocking softly on my door.

"Hey, boss," she says, coming in before I tell her to. "This was just delivered for you. It says private, so I didn't open it."

She's holding a little box with a card. She's clearly curious. As am I.

I take it from her and start to open the card before I realize that she's waiting to see what it is. I raise an eyebrow.

"Thank you," I tell her.

"Oh, no problem," she answers. She stays put, still waiting.

"That will be all," I say, hinting again .

She looks at me.

"Oh!" her eyes widen. "Okay."

She turns around and walks out with a bewildered look on her face. I can understand her confusion. She has practically shared every part of my life since she came here. She takes care of my calendar (including doctor's appointments), and opens all of my mail, including the court papers from the divorce. There has never been anything marked 'Private' before. She's dying to know what it is. And I am too.

I open the card. Bold handwriting is scrawled across a linen card.

Alli Cat,

You said that you weren't sure what you wanted. So I decided that you need to connect with your inner Freak. You need to let loose every once in a while. It's fun. And it's good for you.

Wear this on your date tomorrow night. I will have the remote control with me. Text me where you will be. I'll be there too.

XX,
Shade

I am instantly nervous as I open the little white box. As well I should be.

A long silver egg slides out from the tissue and into my fingers. It is cool to the touch and heavy. I stare at it for a moment before I realize what it is.

It's a vibrator. And it's meant to be worn internally.

Oh, sweet Mary.

I'm shaking my head as though Shade were here with me right now. I'm not wearing this. I'm not doing it.

My phone buzzes.

Have you received my gift?

Shade.

I practically pant now. Both from the gift and from the idea that Shade sent it and expects me to use it.

Yes. I text back. *And there's no way in hell.*

There is a pause. Then a reply.

You'll do it. Because you're daring and fun.

I pause.

Am I? Daring and fun?

Maybe once upon a time, back before Rick the Dick. But being married to him sucked all of the fun out of life. And out of me.

But you're not married to him anymore, I remind myself. Shit. Do I really need to do this to prove that I'm still daring and fun? I mean, I already got a Brazilian wax and had sex with a gigolo. But honestly, in the face of those things, this is a small little thing. Right? It's just a tiny little vibrator. How much of an impact could it possibly make?

I sigh.

Fine. I reply. *I'll do it. I'll text you the info later.*

Think about me this afternoon, he answers.

I shake my head and put my phone away. I can't carry on like this at work. I need to concentrate.

Right after I go to the bathroom and rub a piece of ice on my crotch.

By afternoon, and three pieces of ice later, Bald Brazilian (whom I have affectionately dubbed, BB) is feeling surprisingly better. Apparently the websites that said that the pain should subside within twenty-four hours were right. It doesn't make me less irritated with Sara, but still. It feels good to walk normally and in an upright position again.

Brian, however, is acting strange around me, which is precisely why I didn't want to date someone from work in the first place. And I realize, too, that I haven't gotten to the bottom of how Sara talked him into asking me out.

So I take a little trip to his office, which just so happens to be located on the second floor in Accounting. Like me, he is an Executive Director and has a corner office.

When I walk in, he is sitting with his head buried in a spreadsheet. I sigh.

This is one of the reasons why I know that he and I would never click. He's a numbers guy. I'm a creative girl. I interact with him when I need to get his input on numbers for my projects, but other than that, we don't even move in the same circles. We don't think the same way. Plus, he's got a little coffee stain on his chest.

And yes, I'm a bitch today. But I knew that I would be going into the day. And that probably means that I should call my vagina Bald Bitch, instead. It's ever so much more fitting. Plus, I like it. It makes me feel spunky.

BB and I sit down and I have a little chat with Brian, who is boring, but still nice. I insist that there's no reason to act strangely, that we're just going to dinner as friends. He smiles and acts relieved and then admits that I intimidate him.

"I intimidate you?" I repeat, staring at him in confusion. "Then why in the world would you ask me out?" I pause, then smile. "I forgot. My friend Sara got to you. Tell me, Brian. How exactly did she do that?"

"She friended me online," Brian admits, somewhat sheepishly. "She's very nice."

"Oh, she certainly is," I agree. "Especially when she wants something."

"She said that she just wants you to get out more," Brainy Brian shrugs, smiling his limp smile. "She's worried about you."

I stare at him. Then count to three. "Well, there's no need, is there? You and I are going to dinner tomorrow night. And I'm fine. And I'm looking forward to dinner, by the way. Where would you like to go?"

He looks blank. "I'm not sure," he answers. "What do you like?"

I sigh. I think Shade was right about me. I would really like to date someone who will take charge for a while. I'm sick of having to make all of the decisions, even about something so small as a restaurant.

"How about Manini's on twenty-first street?" I suggest. "I love Italian."

"I do, too," Brian says. His face is contorted in a weird way and I can't really tell if he's smiling or grimacing. I choose to believe that it's a grin. "6:00?"

"That's perfect," I tell him, still staring at him, trying to decide. "I'll just meet you there since I have to be somewhere later that evening."

I leave Brian to his number-crunching.

And by now, now that she isn't on fire anymore, I'm starting to enjoy the smooth feeling of BB when I walk. There might be something to this whole Brazilian thing. I feel sexy as hell knowing that I am completely hairless.

I'm a freaking vixen.

****

I'm a freaking vixen who managed to stay clear of my new boss for the rest of the day.

I am commending myself on that feat as I sit outdoors on my patio waiting for Sara to arrive. I've got four bottles of red Moscato chilling in my fridge at this very moment and I am also making a mental note to buy a wine fridge at my earliest opportunity. It's a necessity in life, really. It's a need, not a want.

I *need* the option of having multiple bottles of wine pre-chilled at any given opportunity for nights just like this. And again, that's a need and not a want. Obviously.

I lie back in the pool lounger and stare up at the dark sky and the glittering white stars. I stare around the tiled pool, at the silent ripples on the water, at the waterfall that feeds into the pool, at the hot-tub that sits slightly above the pool.

Hot tub.

My thoughts freeze, refusing to take another step past the hot tub.

After my day, I obviously deserve to sit in the hot tub. I quickly decide that BB has healed enough that the hot water won't hurt. I also, in my slightly inebriated state, decide that I'm too lazy to make the short walk into my house for a bathing suit. I glance around briefly, deciding that the three foot tall fence provides enough privacy and step out of my clothing.

I leave them in a puddle by my chair and walk buck-ass naked across the stone tiles toward the hot tub. I take a bottle of wine and my glass…the important things. I will worry about unimportant things, like towels, later.

I turn the hot tub on and step in, and the hot water bubbles up and around me, soothing my stress and worry away. The heat doesn't hurt BB at all, which she silently thanks me for.

I am chin-deep in the water when I hear Sara calling for me.

I poke my head up and wave her over.

"I didn't bring my suit," she tells me, standing above me.

"You don't need one," I tell her. "It's only you and me. I've seen you naked a hundred times before." My thoughts are only a bit blurry now after one bottle of wine.

"No?" Sara raises one thin eyebrow. "Two naked women in one hot-tub? What will your neighbors think?"

She obviously doesn't care since she is already stripping off her clothes.

"Well, Mr. Darnell will think that he has won Lady Luck's lottery," I tell her with a grin. "He's always watching Sophie and me when we swim. Perv."

"Speaking of Sophie, where is she?" Sara asks as she settles into the water, across from me. She props one leg up next to me as she sips her wine. I almost tell her that she needs to shave her legs, but decide against it. She might decide that we'll start getting our legs waxed too, which is insanity.

"At Hayley's house," I answer instead, moving away from the stubble on her legs so it doesn't cut me wide open. "They're studying and then she's just going to stay the night. I'm free for the night. I just might sleep out here. Naked."

Sara stares at me again.

"Holy shit. What have I done to you? Are you becoming wild? If so, my work here is done." She makes the sign of the cross on her chest, like she is blessing this event. I roll my eyes.

"Be careful. Your fingers might burst into flame doing that," I smile sweetly before continuing. "After the events of this past week, I've decided that for once, you are right. I've been too uptight for the past...all of my life. I'm going to start not giving a flying eff."

Sara stares at me now. "I think I'm in love with you, girl. Don't marry someone else. After you sow your wild oats, you can marry me."

She laughs, tinkling and loud. I laugh too and fill our wine glasses up. "Nope, can't. I don't like tacos. Remember?"

Sara laughs. "Oh, yeah. I forgot. Details."

Somehow, the next hour passes with lightning speed. During four bottles of wine, I tell Sara all about Shade's little gift, the way Alex had seen my bare crotch, the fact that Alex is strikingly, breathtakingly sexy and the fact that I'm still pissed at her for having Brian ask me out.

"I forgot about being mad at you," I growl, furrowing my eyebrows. Or I think I furrow them. I've had enough wine that my nose and forehead are sort of numb.

"Oh, whatever," Sara waves my concern away. "You know you'll get over it. Because you know that I'm right. You're going to need practice if you're going to date your boss. That's a big step—and it takes skill."

I freeze, staring at her.

"Sara, I am not dating my boss. Not. Gonna. Happen. Please hear me, and don't do anything AT ALL, to try and arrange something like that, okay? I've worked very hard to get to where I'm at. I'm a single woman now- on my own. I can't jeopardize my career simply because the man sets my loins on fire."

I giggle because I use the word 'loins'. And then I glare at her again .

"I'm serious, Sara. I need you to promise me that you won't interfere."

She rolls her eyes. "As if I'd interfere," she croons, stroking my arm. I glare again.

"I mean it."

"Fine," she says, seemingly wounded as she sits back in her seat. "But you underestimate my powers of finesse. I am amazingly subtle."

"Whatever," I roll my eyes again. "You're subtle like an eighteen-wheeler."

At this juncture, my cell phone chooses to ring. I eye the long walk to the table where I left it with my clothes. And I decide that it just isn't worth it.

I take another drink of wine.

And then my phone rings again.

Crap.

"It could be Sophie," I mutter, climbing naked out of my hot-tub and jogging to get it. Unfortunately for me, it's not.

"Alli?"

It's Rick the freaking Dick. I got out of the hot tub for this?

"We need to talk. Vanessa and I are getting married in June. We set the date yesterday. She called Sophie a little bit ago and asked Sophie to be a bridesmaid and your daughter screamed at her. And then hung up on her. You need to talk to her."

"To Vanessa?" I'm confused. It might be the effects of the wine. I'm not sure. And it might also be the effects of the wine, but a little part of me is shocked and somewhat sad that Rick has already set a date. I don't want him- that much is certain, but to know that he would rush out so quickly and get re-married, it's a little hurtful. Like I didn't matter at all.

"No, Allison," Rick sighs. "To Sophie. You need to explain to her that it is important that she participate in my wedding."

And I'm done feeling hurt. It was a short-lived excursion from reality, anyway.

"What? I'm not talking to Sophie about this. If you want her in your wedding, you can pick up the phone and call your daughter yourself. Stop letting the women in your life take care of everything. She's your daughter— you need a relationship with her. And that includes talking to her."

"Why do you have to be such a bitch, Allison?" Rick snaps. "I'm just asking for a little help. I don't think that's too much to ask, considering that I haven't filed a lawsuit after you tried to run over my fiancée."

And now I'm pissed. I step back into the hot-tub since I'm shivering.

"Are you insane? I'm being a bitch? And you really feel like you could have filed a lawsuit? If that's really what you want to do, do it!" I snap. "I don't need you thinking that you did me a favor by not. Your lawyer already tried to contact me about this anyway."

"I told him to back off," Rick says. "But I could just as easily call him back and tell him to proceed."

I'm sputtering, trying to decide what to say when Sara butts in.

"Give me the phone," she slurs. I yank away, but she manages to get my phone first.

"Listen, you small-dicked asshole. You deserve to marry a gold-digging whore. And I'm going to do everything in my power to make sure that Sophie is nowhere near your wedding. And your twig-legged little bitch could have dented Alli's car. She should sue *you* for that." Small pause. "Hell, yes, this is Sara! Who the fuck else would it be? Do not call Alli again with this kind of bull-shit."

I try to grab the phone away from her and she wrenches away.

"I mean it, Rick. She doesn't answer to you. And she doesn't have to help you anymore. Handle your own shit."

And she hangs up on him. She lays my phone on the tiles and turns to me.

"Don't let him talk to you like that anymore," she instructs me. "He doesn't have the right."

I'm staring at her speechless when my phone rings again.

Fire flares up in Sara's eyes and she yanks my phone to her ear.

"You want more, Tiny Dick? Leave her alone. Only contact her through a lawyer from now on. She's SO over you- she doesn't even want to hear your voice. In fact, she's so over you that she's dating again, too. For your info, her new boss is sexy and fabulous and fucking rich. You'll never be able to compare."

Pause.

Another pause.

Sara's eyes widen and she hands me the phone. She is speechless which is terrifying, in itself. I look at her questioningly as I lift the phone to my ear.

"Hello?"

"Allison?"

Oh, holy shit. I want to effing die.

It's Alex.

It's time to hyperventilate.

Chapter Eleven

(Or: A Woman can't survive on Embarrassment Alone)

"Um. Hi, Alex."

"Hi, Allison." My new boss sounds unsure of himself and I'm not sure what to say.

"Tell him your friend is insane!" Sara screeches into my ear.

I wave her away.

"I'm sorry about that," I tell him as calmly as I can. "My friend and I are having wine, probably too much of it, and my ex-husband called a minute ago. My friend was worked up and obviously when you called, she thought it was him calling back. I'm so sorry about the confusion."

I think I pull it off. I sound cool and confident.

Alex laughs, a buttery-rich sound in my ear.

"It's okay. I've been around wine and women before. I get it. And I'm glad I can be of assistance with your ex-husband. He's apparently quite the treat."

I breathe a sigh of relief. It doesn't look like I'm going to get fired over this.

"I'm sorry to call you so late, anyway," he continues. "I was just thinking about what I said to you earlier after your staff meeting and I decided that it was inappropriate and wanted to apologize. I sincerely hope that I didn't offend you. But now I'm thinking that since your friend called me a Tiny Dick, we might be even."

He laughs and, no lie, a shiver runs down my spine. I may want to take a bath in his laugh. Then shove it against the wall and have violent sex with it. And I should probably not drink this much wine ever again.

"It's not a problem," I tell him. "I told you, I don't offend easily. I apologize for this morning, too, by the way. I could explain the whole situation, but it wouldn't really be appropriate. Let's just say that I don't usually come to work with no underwear. Can we leave it at that?"

Alex laughs again. "Of course. I think working with you is going to be very interesting," he answers, chuckling.

"I'm sorry," I tell him again. "I promise, I'm usually very professional."

"Don't be sorry," he tells me firmly. "I told you, I like employees with spunk. We're going to be a great team. Have a good night, Allison."

He hangs up.

And I turn and glare at Sara.

"Is there any other aspect of my life you would like to try and wreck? Maybe you'd like to buy Sophie a gigolo and get her pregnant or something?"

Sara actually looks pained.

"I'm sorry, Alli," she says quietly. "I truly didn't mean to do that. I thought it was Rick."

I sigh.

"I know. And you were just trying to be a good friend. But damn girl, with a friend like you, who needs enemies?"

I fill our glasses back up with the last of the wine and we sit back, our heads leaned together. Sara picks up her leg and starts counting the stars with her toe.

"You'd better stay here tonight," I tell her. "You shouldn't drive."

"You've got that right, sister," she mumbles.

I can tell from her super relaxed face that I need to get her out of the hot tub, pronto, before she falls asleep. And that is what leads to the fact that I am hoisting her naked body out of the water when Mr. Darnell goes into his backyard to take his trash out.

At this point in the day, I don't even care. I just wave over my shoulder, ignoring his flabbergasted expression, as I help Sara into my house.

We're both naked and dripping wet.

This day just can't get any worse.

And nobody should ever say that. Because what always happens when they do?

Things get worse.

That's right.

Well, not exactly worse, but definitely uncomfortable. And slightly hilarious (in hindsight).

Sigh.

Because I was so tired, after I dropped Sara onto one side of my bed and covered her up, I laid down for just a second on the other side. For just for one second.

But apparently, when two people split four bottles of wine, it does something to their sense of time. Because when I open my eyes, it is morning and Sophie is standing over me.

"'Morning, honey," I mumble. She raises an eyebrow.

"I guess it is," she says. "But not as good as last night, apparently. Why are you and Aunt Sara naked together in your bed?"

Eff.

I sit straight up and look at Sara. She is sleeping soundly, snoring softly, with drool pooling on my expensive brushed Egyptian cotton sheets.

And she is naked.

And I am naked.

I sigh.

"Obviously, it's not what it looks like," I tell Sophie as I jab Sara in the ribs.

"Of course not," Sophie giggles, as she turns to walk out of the room. "Have a good day, mom. I just came by to pick up my math book. You'd better hurry. You're going to be late for work."

I look at the clock and then leap from the bed, yanking all of Sara's covers off in the process.

I only have fifteen minutes to get ready. Effffffffff.

"Sara!" I yell as I head for the bathroom. "Get up. We're late."

She sits up and looks around bewilderedly. "Did we get drunk and drive to Vegas and get married?"

I laugh as I start the shower. "You're half right. We got drunk, you cussed out Rick the Dick and then called my new boss a Tiny Dick. And we *live* in Vegas."

She looks shocked, then she smiles at me. "Well, then. You're just lucky your best friend is such a bad ass."

I sigh.

"Get your bad ass in Sophie's shower. We're going to be late."

She laughs and stumbles down the hall as I jump in the shower and try to figure out how I'm going to look Alex in the face today.

****

It's not as hard as one might think.

And it's certainly not as hard as I thought it was going to be.

Alex is acting like everything is perfectly normal.

He brought me another cup of gourmet coffee and left it on my desk with a note.

This is me, starting over.
Have a great day, AH

I have to smile at that and I am still smiling as Taylor walks in with a bunch of papers that need my signature.

"Why are you smiling like that?" she asks suspiciously. "Are people getting laid off today?"

I stare at her in horror. "Of course not! And why would I be smiling about that?"

She shrugs as she sets the folders down in front of me and settles into a chair to wait.

"I don't know. You've been a little, shall we say...edgy lately. People have noticed. Everyone is asking me what your deal is."

Hell.

I sigh.

"I don't have a deal," I tell her as I pick up a pen and start sifting through the stack. "I've just had an interesting week and I might be in a weird mood. I'm sorry."

She stares at me. "What *has* been going on?" she asks curiously. "Tonya told me that you're going out with Brian tonight. I told her that in no way was that true, but she said that Brian told her himself."

I restrain myself from shuddering. And I can't deny it since Tonya is Brian's assistant.

"It's true," I admit sadly. "We're having dinner as friends tonight. We're both divorced so we thought it might be nice to get together with someone who understands what we're going through. As *friends.*"

"Thank god," Taylor breathes. "I thought you had lost your mind."

I sign my name to a document and glance up at her.

"Nope. My mind is intact. Probably."

She laughs and I laugh with her. She has no idea of the lengths my sanity has gone to this week.

"And what's the deal with Alex bringing you coffee?" she asks. "Our old VP never even came out of his office. Alex has brought you coffee twice *and* he gets here before you in the morning. He's probably going to start getting mad that you're not here when he stops by."

I don't even look up.

"I'm sure he's just a different breed of VP," I tell her. "He's energetic and progressive, unlike the old regime here. I personally think he's a breath of fresh air."

"I'm glad to hear it," his voice says from the door.

I look up and my heart has palpitations.

I should have said that he's a stunningly handsome breath of fresh air.

Because he is.

He's dressed in a black suit today, with a white button-up, loosened at the neck and no tie. He manages to look formal, yet casual. He's got classic handsome features and his eyes seem like they can stare right into my soul.

I have to make myself remember to breathe.

And then to answer him.

"Hi Alex," I say brightly. "Thank you for the coffee."

"Anytime," he answers, coming in and sitting in the chair next to Taylor. She fidgets, obviously uncomfortable that he heard her question his behavior. He notices and turns to her.

"Taylor, right?" he asks kindly. She nods. "I'm an early riser. I get here before anyone else does. In fact, I'm the first one here. It's just habit and I certainly don't expect anyone else to arrive that early. So, no worries."

He smiles at her and I can see the relief flood Taylor's face. Along with appreciation of his sexiness. The man oozes sexuality and power and grace. It's intoxicating. Even for me, a jaded, middle-aged divorcee. Then my thoughts pause for a moment. Is thirty-five middle aged? Holy hell. My thoughts are appalled. But I'm brought back to the present when Alex turns to me.

"Do you have just a second? I need to run something past you."

"Of course," I answer, handing Taylor the stack of signed documents. She takes them and leaves, closing my door behind her. "Thank you for handling that so gracefully.   Taylor's   an   excellent   assistant.   She's just...inquisitive."

Alex smiles. "And you're a good boss."

I can't help but smile back. I happen to have the God of Business sitting across from me, looking all sexy and perfect and filling my office with his oozing sex appeal. If I did anything but smile back at him, I'd be insane. He could probably fire me and I'd smile at this point. But surely that's not the thing that he wanted to run past me. To be on the safe side, I ask.

"So, what is this thing that you want to run past me?"

He settles back into his chair, making himself more comfortable as he crosses one ankle over his thigh.

"I've been playing with an idea. I know I'm new, but this thing has been nagging at me. We're a shoe company. We've always been a shoe company. But I have an idea...to co-produce a product with a distributor that I know. A custom-fit shoe insert for athletes. We'd capitalize on the Zeller shoe brand and use that consumer trust that has already been established to launch this product. It's a great way to diversify without going out of our comfort zone too far. What do you think?"

I stare at him, impressed.

"It's so simple that it's brilliant," I admit. "We need another product in our arsenal. Have you run this past R&D?"

He's already shaking his head. "Not yet. I'd like to go and get the specifics so that we can build up a cost analysis and a risk portfolio before we pitch it. I've got an appointment next week to meet with the distributor and

I'd like for you to come with me. We can probably wrap up the trip in two days or so. Can you make it work?"

I nod. "Of course. Thank you for your confidence in me. I appreciate that you brought me in on this project."

He smiles. "I told you...we're going to make a great team."

I feel warm inside for a minute. This man's smile melts my internal organs. I decide that I should get hazard pay for working with him before I return his smile.

"Yes," I tell him. "We are."

And before I can stop it, my thoughts run away from me. I picture his full lips blazing a trail across my neck, down over my collarbone and stopping at my breasts before he sucks there, and then bending me over his desk... and then....

"Allison?"

I snap to attention and my cheeks flare with color.

"Yes?"

"Are you alright? You look flushed."

I nod quickly and stand.

"I'm fine. I think I just need some breakfast. Have a good morning, Alex."

I walk out and fight the urge to make a trip to the lounge and put my head in the freezer to cool off. I'm insane. I'm an insane, randy, middle-aged woman who just fantasized about her boss while sitting with him.

But to be fair, Alex Harris is a man who was just made to fantasize about.

I can't control Mother Nature.

****

As sexy as Alex Harris is, my thoughts are far from him later that night as I prepare for my date with Brainy Brian.

And I've seriously got to stop calling him that. I don't want to accidentally reply to him with, 'I'm sorry, I didn't catch that, Brainy.' I shake my head and roll my eyes. He might be boring and I don't see anything coming of our dating, but I don't want to offend him. He's a sweet guy and he can't help being boring.

And even though I'm having dinner with him, it's Shade who I am dressing for.

I study myself in the mirror.

I'm a freaking siren tonight. I've pulled out all stops.

I'm wearing a black cocktail dress, snug in all the right places, which falls to a soft stop two inches above my knee. I'm wearing black thigh-high stockings and killer black Fuck-Me-Pumps. Seriously, these shoes, with their four-inch stilettos, steal the show. They might have been $900, but as far as I'm concerned, they were worth every penny.

I slide some bright red lipstick on and examine the finished product. My hair cascades over my shoulders, my smoky eyes are perfect... and well, smoky. I personally think that smoky eyes are the sexiest of all eyes. I look great. Even I have to admit that. And knowing that makes me feel sexy.

I dab on some vanilla based perfume, because I read somewhere, once upon a time, that men love it. Supposedly, vanilla is supposed to be an aphrodisiac. And I know I'm paying Shade, but still. I'd like for him to be turned on, too.

And why am I worrying about this? The guy is in his twenties. I'm sure he doesn't have problems in that area yet.

I am transferring stuff from my regular purse into a sleek, black evening purse when my phone buzzes. Shade.

Are you wearing it?

Shit.

I had been putting off inserting that sleek silver egg so much so that I had literally forgotten it. Hell.

I will be in a minute.

I put my phone down and hunt for the little white box that I had hidden in my bed-stand. I open it up and stare at the innocuous metallic toy.

It looks harmless.

So why does it terrify me?

Because deep down, I'm a prude, that's why.

Yes, I have slept with a gigolo this week and used a vibrator, but those were first time occurrences after a lifetime of being a prude. Old habits die hard. But I am determined to change them. I'm the new and improved Allison, the one with no fear. The one whose young lover calls her Alli Cat. I'm invincible. Alli Cat the Invincible. Practically a super hero, really.

I smile at that and pick up the little egg, trotting off for the bathroom.

Thinking of me in that way, like Shade does with himself when he separates himself and Colby, makes it easier. During the day, I'm Allison. I'm responsible and hard-working and ambitious.

But at night, when I'm not at work, I'm Alli Cat. I'm fierce and daring and fun. And I have a freaking bald vagina. BB is fun, too.

Holy shit.

My fingers tremble as I slide the little silver bullet into BB.

I stand upright and assess the situation.

I can feel it in there, a slight weight leaning against my pelvic floor. But after a moment, I'm used to it and I can't feel it anymore. It's like a metallic tampon. My body absorbed the sensation and now it's like it isn't even there.

But I'm sure, as soon as Shade presses a button, it will announce its presence again loud and clear.

I gulp as I pick up my phone again.

Okay, I'm wearing it.

Shade's answer is immediate.

Good. I can't test it because I'm out of range. But I'll be at Manini's soon. Your mission tonight is to orgasm while at the table with your date—and to not let him know.

I gulp. Seriously?

But even as I am hesitant, a little thrill of excitement shoots through me, too. It feels so naughty. Because it is so naughty. And you know what that means? I truly am daring and fun. I'm no longer boring Allison who stayed married to a loser for too many years. I'm Alli Cat the Invincible now. And I'm freaking fun.

I grab my purse and head out the door.

Chapter Twelve

(Or: The Education of Alli Cat)

Manini's is a great restaurant for a date, which is why I chose it.

It is dimly lit, romantic and quiet. The only downside is that they have great bread which is drizzled in garlic-butter. And that is a downside because I have to find the strength to not eat it since I'll be kissing Shade later.

But I have amazing fortitude, I remind myself. I can do this.

I can also get through Brainy Brian's oh-so-boring small talk.

Because I have fortitude.

"So, I recently joined a dating site," he tells me as he chews on a piece of bread. I eye his half-eaten bread longingly. It doesn't even matter to me that he's been chewing on it with his fish-lips.

"Really?" I ask politely, picking up my glass of wine delicately by the stem and sipping it. In actuality, I'd like to slam it down on the side of the table and use the jagged shards to slit my wrist. But I paste on a smile to hide those suicidal thoughts. "How's that going?"

"Oh, so far, so good," Brian answers. "I haven't gotten any replies to my ad yet, but I'm contacting a few women. I think I would recommend it to you…when you're ready to start dating for real, that is."

He smiles and I am reminded that he truly is a nice person. And I feel guilty for wanting to open a vein a moment ago.

"I don't know when I'll be ready for that, but I appreciate the tip," I tell him.

I cross my legs and as I do, I feel a startling jolt, then a flood of intense pleasure as the egg situated inside of BB starts buzzing.

Holy shit.

I snap to attention in my seat, trying hard to act casual and nonchalant, even though the vibrations feel so freaking good. I gaze around the room for Shade.

I find him sitting in the shadows in a booth a short distance away. He's staring at me, his blue, blue eyes intense as he watches me squirm.

He releases the button. I know this because the buzzing stops. My uterine muscles relax from where they were glued to my abdominal ceiling.

Shade smiles angelically at me. I take a deep breath and turn back around.

Brian is staring at me.

"Are you alright?" he asks in concern.

I smile.

"Of course. I'm fine. Just a little cramp in my leg."

And by that, I mean a convulsion in my uterus.

We continue conversing with Brian's idea of small-talk. He is thrilling me with the reasons why the General

Ledger didn't balance last month at work when Shade hits the button again.

I almost go through the roof this time, because my nerves are still on high-alert from the first time.

I inhale shakily and try to get a hold of myself as I grip the edges of the table so tightly that my knuckles turn white.

As the buzzing threatens to send me over the edge this time and I struggle to look normal, I waver between hating Shade and loving him. This is an excruciating pain/pleasure. And it's exciting as hell because everyone around me is going on with dinner as usual because they have no idea that I'm on the verge of having an orgasm in my seat.

Shade releases the button and I release the edge of the table.

Oh my Lord.

I breathe out slowly.

I glance at Shade, with a tiny glare, and he smiles beatifically again.

Freaking punk.

As if he read my mind, Shade pushes the button again immediately.

And I arch against the table. My uterus is screaming as it threatens to contract me right into an orgasm. I'm practically panting as Brian continues to talk in his boring monotone.

And then the waiter comes to take our main dish order.

I expect Shade to relent, to release the button.

But he doesn't.

In fact, as I'm getting ready to bite out my order, he increases the speed.

I cry out and both the waiter and Brian stare at me in concern.

"Are you alright?" Brian asks again. I nod, unable to speak.

I take a deep breath and try again.

"Fine. I'd. Like. Pasta Alfredo." I'm speaking stiltedly, but I can't help it. They're just lucky that I'm not screaming right now. Holy shit. I'm going to come with both of them staring at me.

I grip the table as the waiter takes Brian's order.

"I'll. Be right. Back," I manage to eke out.

I spring from the table and practically sprint for the ladies room.

The entire way, the egg is buzzing along nicely, doing its job to drive me to the brink of madness. As I'm closing the door, it is pushed open and Shade stands there. The remote control is dangling from his hand. He releases the button, and the agonizing/amazing vibrations stop. He locks the door.

Then drops the remote.

He falls to his knees and shoves up my skirt, nuzzling my inner thigh. I bury my hands in his hair.

"You're a devil," I tell him raggedly as he licks my freaking clit. Then he pulls out my egg and drops it with the remote.

"I wanted to feel you come rather than watch it," he tells me as pushes me against the wall. I hear the rustling of foil again and then Shade is sliding into me, long and thick and full.

Holy Freaking Hell.

I'm ready for him because of the egg. No further foreplay is necessary.

And I'm having sex in a public bathroom.

It's a very clean and fancy public bathroom, but still.

And it doesn't matter.

"Do you know how sexy you are?" Shade murmurs in my ear as he nibbles at it.

He is surging against me, the muscles of his torso pushing me into the wall and it is an exquisite, sensual feeling. His hands curve around until they are cupping my ass, pulling me to him.

Because of the egg, I come in two minutes flat.

I fall limply against Shade as he tenses, then relaxes.

He just came.

I stare at him.

"Do you come with all of your clients?"

The question is out before I even know it. Because honestly, I don't want to know about his other clients.

He grins down at me as he peels off the condom and drops it into the trash. His thighs might as well be chiseled from marble. That is how muscled he is. My eyes are glued to them as he pulls up his trousers and fastens them.

"I'm a guy, Alli Cat," he answers. "I can pretty much come anytime, anywhere."

For now, I think silently, remembering how Rick the Dick started having problems with that as he got older. But I don't tell Shade. He'll figure it out in about fifteen years.

"Now, part two of your mission is to go back out there and have dinner like nothing ever happened," Shade tells me. "You can do it. You are daring and fun."

"I am daring and fun," I repeat firmly as I pull my skirt down and straighten my hair.

"Then, you will join me at Utopia after dinner. I have a surprise planned for you tonight."

He grins wickedly and I am instantly apprehensive.

"Another surprise? I'm old, Shade. I don't know that my heart can take two surprises in one day."

I'm only half-joking.

Shade laughs. "You're not old. You're in your sexual prime. And so am I. Let's use that to our advantage, shall we?"

Well, hell. If he wants to put it that way.

I return to Brian's table and apologize. I explain that I had a sudden headache onset, but that I took some aspirin in the bathroom and that I'm feeling better already. I eat the entire bowl of pasta, feeling certain that I'm going to need the carbs as fuel for the rest of my evening with Shade.

****

It turns out that I was oh-so-very correct. I needed those carbs.

Shade meets me at the curb of Utopia. Under the neon signs of the street, I am stricken once again by how very handsome he is. Holy hell. He is strong and tall and confident. His face is absolutely, perfectly chiseled. Once again, he leads me through the back hallways of the club to a quiet room.

After we enter, Shade pulls me into his arms, kissing me roughly.

"I've been thinking about you for the past hour," he admits to me. "That was sexy as hell, Alli Cat."

And it was, I have to admit. My knees actually still feel a little weak from our little escapade in the restaurant.

I let his tongue explore my mouth, my neck, my breasts, as he pulls the straps of my dress down and licks at my nipples. I bury my hands in his hair once again. He's got thick dark hair. It's every bit as soft as it looks, too.

He pulls away.

"Tonight, I'm going to do you a favor," he tells me. "I know you'll be dating again soon. A sexy woman like you isn't going to sit at home alone for long."

I start to say something, but he puts a finger to my lips.

"And I want you to be prepared. I already know that you like to be good at everything you do. It's in your nature. So, tonight, I'm going to show you exactly what will drive a man wild. And you're going to enjoy the lesson."

My lips curve into a smile. He's very perceptive, this one. He's already got me pegged.

"So, you're going to turn me into a sex goddess?" I ask with a grin.

He smiles back as he pulls me to him.

"You already are a sex goddess," he tells me. "I'm going to turn you into a very skilled sex goddess who can bring a man to his knees in five minutes flat."

I smile wider. "I'm going to enjoy tonight," I answer.

"Oh, me too," he says confidently, winking before he continues.

"Okay. First, to set the scenario. You're going to pretend that I'm a guy who you have been dating and you are very into me. This is 'the night'. The first night that you have sex. And you're going to take total and complete charge because that's sexy as hell. And I'm going to tell you what to do. I don't want you to argue—just do everything I say and commit it to memory. Can you do that?"

I nod, a slow grin forming again. "Of course. I have an excellent memory."

"I'll bet you do," Shade grins back. "You are at your date's house...my house. You are sitting in the living room, having a glass of wine. Tell me that you're going to change into something more comfortable. Then walk into his bedroom and find one of his dress shirts in his closet. Take off your bra and leave on your panties. Take off your stockings and leave on your heels. Unbutton the shirt until the curve of your breast is visible. Then walk back out here very confidently and stand in front of me."

"Done." I turn on my heel and start to walk away.

"Wait," Shade calls. "You didn't tell me anything."

Crap. I turn around.

"I'm going to change into something a little more comfortable," I tell him. I smile what I hope is a sexy grin. Shade nods.

"Make yourself at home," he answers, grinning back.

I slip into the bathroom and look around. The bathroom is incredibly nice, filled with marble and granite and pewter fixtures. There is also a closet. I open it and lo and behold, there is a dress shirt hanging there.

I smile and slip it from the hanger.

I do exactly what Shade told me. I unbutton the shirt until I can see the curve of my breast in the mirror. I tousle my hair so that I look sexy. I peel off my stockings and leave on my underwear, but put my heels back on.

Shade has moved to the couch in the sitting area of the room. He is sitting with his legs crossed and is sipping a glass of wine. He's perfectly in character.

He stares at me as I emerge from the bathroom.

"You look beautiful," he tells me quietly. "Come here."

I walk toward him, expecting him to want me on his lap. But when I get a few feet in front of him, he says, "Stop."

I stop.

"Now stand there for a moment. Look me in the eye."

I do.

He stares at me.

"Be confident," he instructs.

My chin comes up and I jut my hips out.

A grin slowly spreads over Shade's face.

"That's perfect. Men like to look," he explains. "And women don't usually like to be looked at. They feel vulnerable, exposed. They are self-conscious about their perceived flaws. What they don't understand is that men don't see them the same way they see themselves. We see curves and we *love* those curves. Confidence is sexy as hell, Alli Cat. It's the sexiest possible thing that you can wear."

Holy shit. I remember when Sara told me that very same thing. Was she actually right about something?

"Now, walk straight over here, maintaining eye contact. Straddle me and kiss me thoroughly."

So, I do. His mouth tastes like vodka, tonic and lime. His large hands cup my ass and pull me into him so that I'm grinding against his muscle. I can feel the dampness of my panties as I straddle his crotch.

"Now, flip around."

I stare at him, confused.

"Throw one leg over and turn around on my lap," he tells me. "And grind for just a moment more."

I am still confused, but I do what he says.

His breathing is a little labored when he says, "Now, stand up."

I stand up, directly in front of him.

"Bend over."

Without hesitation, I bend over.

I feel slightly ridiculous, but I can hear Shade breathing. He likes this. He's looking at my ass, I can tell. So, I cross one knee over the over and stick it out just a little further.

"Men love the way a woman's ass is framed by her panties," he tells me. "It's always nice to see it. Women are usually so fast to throw their panties off and dive under the covers."

He reaches up and grabs my ass. "And you've got a fine ass."

I smile.

"Now, step away from me, turn and take off your panties. Toss them into my lap. Maintain eye contact with me the entire time."

I follow his instructions word for word. And oddly, even though he is directing me, I feel solidly in control. Shade's eyes are glued to my every movement. Everything that I am doing is something that I know he is enjoying. The evidence is in the way his pants are straining at his crotch and the way he is breathing so harshly.

I like it.

My panties are now in his lap.

"Sit on my lap again."

So I do. Shade's hands run over my back, down my hips and grab my bare ass as he kisses me. His tongue explores every inch of my mouth before he sucks on the base of my neck.

I am grinding into his hardness and his hands pull me ever closer.

He whispers into my ear, "Now stand up and slowly unbutton your shirt. Slip it off, but tease me for a second-hold it to your breasts, as if you're unsure whether to reveal yourself. Then drop it to the ground. Stand there without moving, with your shoulders back and your chin out. Be confident and let me look at you."

"Yes," I say simply. I stand up and do what he says.

As I stand and let him look at me, my skin is on fire. I'm not sure who is more turned on, him or me.

After he looks at me for a couple of minutes and I see the desire in his eyes, he speaks again. His voice is husky and rich.

"Most women think that in order for them to take charge in the bedroom, they need to be on top. I personally don't prefer women on top. I think most men would agree. I'm always a little nervous that you're going to miscalculate and crush my dick. Instead, you can be in control, but still let *me* feel in control and that is sexy as hell."

"How?" I ask softly, licking my lips.

"Walk over here and bend down. Whisper into my ear that you want me to fuck you now."

I walk over, even with my knees weakening by the moment, and bend. I flick my tongue out and lick him lightly at the base of his ear, inhaling his delicious scent.

"I want you to fuck me now," I tell him. I am so happy that I have already practiced saying that word at home. It makes it much easier to say now in front of him.

"Men like naughty words," he says simply. "Grab my hand and lead me to the bed. When we get there, you can kick off your shoes."

We make our way to the bed.

I kick off my shoes as directed.

"Now tell me to fuck you."

"Fuck me," I breathe into his ear, before I kiss him heatedly again. He inhales my tongue and bends me back onto the bed. He strips his clothes off in thirty-seconds flat and quickly rolls a condom on. Before I know it, his warm skin is sliding against me. I wrap my legs around him and pull him close."

"Tell me you love my cock."

"I love your cock," I whisper into his neck.

He quickens his pace and slides in and out; hard, then harder. Then he slows.

"Tell me to fuck you harder."

"Fuck me harder," I murmur.

So he does. The muscles of his back ripple and strain as he bucks against me. His skin is damp and his dick is hard. I grasp at his shoulders, holding on.

"Now, tell me to stop."

"What??" I look at him wildly. "I don't want you to stop."

Shade grins lazily as he hovers above me. "I don't particularly want to stop. But I know that if you do this next thing, it will make this sex mind-blowing and that's what you want, right?"

I nod.

"So, tell me to stop."

"Stop."

"Now, I want you to roll me to the side and suck me. I know that women's magazines like to tell women to take men to the brink, to almost make them come and then stop because it will make the orgasm more intense. But that's not true. Usually, it's only frustrating. Unless you are doing it this way. This way is amazing."

I follow his instructions. I feel kinky as hell, because let's face it, it is kinky as hell. But I suck him. And yes, I taste myself.

He moves with me, pushing into me. It only takes a couple of minutes before he says, "I'm ready to come.

Stop. Come up here and kiss me. Then tell me to bend you over and fuck you."

I wipe my mouth and straighten.

I kiss him. "Bend me over and fuck me," I tell him softly, against his lips.

"With pleasure," he says. He bends me over the bed and easily slides in, then out. Hard, harder, harder.

"Tell me to come in you."

"You're wearing a condom," I point out raggedly.

"It doesn't matter. It's just sexy as hell to hear." He sounds equally ragged.

"Come in me," I say.

"Done," he answers harshly. And he leans into my ass, pushing against me, grasping my hips.

Holy effing shit.

He shudders for a moment, then he's still.

"That was hot as hell," I tell him as I collapse onto the bed.

Shade looks at me knowingly as he collapses next to me, his handsome face smug.

"Yep. And now you are the master of mind-blowing sex. You're welcome."

"Thank you," I laugh, snuggling into his side. His arm wraps around me and pulls me close and suddenly, it doesn't feel like we're client and clientele. I feel like we just had an amazing sexual experience. It was mutually amazing and he enjoyed it as much as I did.

He's very, very good at his job.

Chapter Thirteen

(Or: I am Cougar, Hear me roar while I do a jello shot)

The sun is out, the Las Vegas sky is blue and Shade has his hands all over my daughter.

Okay, not in *that* way, but still.

I am lying poolside in a bright yellow bikini top and cut-off denim shorts watching Colby and Sophie's lesson. He's currently showing her how to make her butterfly more efficient. And as he does, every muscle in his chest is flexing. If Sophie weren't here, I would jump into my pool fully clothed and lick each ripple.

But she *is* here.

And so I'm in mom mode. And Shade is Colby.

And I'm not really liking the fact that his hands are balancing her in the water right now as she practices.

Does that make me jealous of my own daughter?

Have I fallen down a freaking rabbit hole?

I sigh and take a sip of lemonade. Which is sans vodka, by the way, and that is a true tragedy considering the circumstances.

Since it's only 3:15 p.m. on a Saturday, I decided to hold off on the alcohol for a bit. Particularly since Rick the Dick will be coming to pick Sophie up for the night here in a bit. I should probably be stone-cold sober for that.

I really do have amazing fortitude.

"Sophie, pick up your chin!" Colby calls as Sophie butterflies across the pool. From here, she looks like a very skinny porpoise. Colby glances at me, and his gaze turns wicked. He actually winks as his gaze slides down over my chest, then back up to my eyes.

Butterflies of my own flutter in my stomach.

His expression is playful and naughty as he climbs from the pool and walks to me, bending down to grab the towel next to me.

"Are we on for next weekend?" he asks quietly, staring down at me with his blue, blue, blue freaking eyes.

I smile. "I don't know," I answer. "It's still *this* weekend. Next weekend is a long way away."

He chuckles, glancing over his shoulder to make sure Sophie is still swimming. She is.

"Ah, don't tease me, Alli Cat. I'm going to need my Alli fix by next weekend. And you're going to need Shade."

I swallow. He's actually right. I will definitely need Shade by next weekend. It's a thought that has already crossed my mind and it's a little bothersome. Have I come to depend on him already…to fill up my alone time? It's a slightly troublesome thought.

"Maybe," I answer coyly, hiding my concern.

He grins. "I'll schedule you in for a block of time," he tells me. "Just in case." And he winks again as he towels off his hair. God, I love it when he winks. It's so cute and ornery. And flirty.

I am still looking up at him when I hear Rick the Dick's voice coming through the gate.

Hell.

I stand up and Colby walks over to Sophie, presumably to give her some last tips before she has to leave with her dad.

Rick comes over to me, his gaze sliding up and down my body. I try not to shudder. The thought that this slime-ball's hands have been on my body so many times throughout the last fifteen years is enough to make me want to drown myself in my own pool, right after I fill it with acid, of course, to burn off the memory of his touch.

"You're looking good, Alli," he tells me. Even his voice is disgusting to me now. "You're working out."

"I've always worked out, Rick," I remind him sharply. "You just never noticed. It's hard to notice your wife when you've always got a girlfriend on the side."

He doesn't appear to hear my barb.

He steps closer. "Yes, you do look good." At his words, he actually runs his thumb along my elbow. I yank away, then stand in shock, staring at him.

"What the hell, Rick?" I demand. "Don't touch me."

Rick just stares at me, then laughs. "And there's the ice queen that I divorced. *Don't touch me, Rick. Not tonight, Rick. I have a migraine, Rick.* And you wonder why I went outside of our marriage to get fulfillment? It's because you never satisfied me, Allison. A man needs fulfillment."

I stare at him, in utter shock and disgust.

"Somehow, Rick, that's not the way I remember it at all. In fact, I remember having sex two or three times a week, many of those times when I was drop-dead tired, but I never complained. I remember going away for weekends- just the two of us- where we had plentiful sex.

I even thought it was good sex at the time, but since you've been gone, I've discovered that sex with you was never good. I just didn't know any better. But I do now. You can't blame your cheating ways on me. It's your fault, not mine."

Rick stares at me calmly, seemingly unfazed by my biting words.

"You know, when you get bitchy, the crow's feet around your eyes really start to show up. You should avoid doing that if you want to hide the tired hag that you actually are."

I am beyond pissed now, but by this point, Sophie has climbed out of the water and is coming our way. I know that I can't say anything in reply and Rick knows it too. He smirks at me.

Colby walks behind Sophie, his eyes on my face. He can tell that I'm agitated. He narrows his eyes.

"Daddy!" Sophie calls. "Did you see my Butterfly?"

Rick gives me one last glare before turning around.

"Yes, I did. It's coming along famously. And this must be the swim coach I'm paying for."

Ugh. Leave it to Rick to reduce everything to money. How did I stay with him for so long? I want to literally slap myself in the forehead.

"Hello, sir," Colby says, sticking out his hand. "I'm Colby. And yes, I'm the swim coach. Your daughter is doing fabulously. I think you'll be pleased at her progress."

"I'm sure," Rick says coolly. He shakes Colby's hand, but briefly. Then he turns to Sophie, very pointedly ignoring Colby by turning his back on him.

And I know why.

Rick is a very shallow, very insecure man. Being in the presence of a young and amazingly fit and handsome guy like Colby is wreaking havoc on Rick's self-confidence. Particularly since Colby is still in his swim trunks. There's not an ounce of fat on him and he's got a rippling six-pack across his abdomen. And I know for a fact that Rick has a beer gut that he is very, very self-conscious of. Colby is tall and lean and beautiful and Rick is aging as we speak. This situation almost makes up for Rick's jab about my crow's feet.

Almost.

"Sophie, let's go get your stuff. Vanessa is waiting for us- we've got dinner reservations in town."

And they turn and walk away. Rick doesn't say another thing to me and enters my house like it is still his own. I grit my teeth.

"Are you alright?" Colby asks, glancing at my face. "Your ex is a real asshat."

I smile at the term. "Yes, he is. Now imagine being married to that piece of asshat for the past fifteen years."

Colby shakes his head. "Temporary insanity?"

He grins.

"Can fifteen years be classified as temporary?" I answer.

Colby shrugs. "I guess it depends on perspective. If you look at the long scheme of things, then fifteen years is temporary if you're looking at an entire lifespan. Just think. If you had played your cards right, you could still be with that gem."

I shudder. Literally shudder. Colby laughs and puts his hand on my arm.

"But you're not with him. Because you played your cards right. And here you are with me."

Yes, because I'm paying you, I think. But I don't say that. I smile instead.

"You're right. I should most definitely count my blessings. Would you like a beer or something? I'm going in to say goodbye to Sophie, but I'll be back in a second."

Colby smiles. "I have no place to be," he announces. "I had a cancelation for tonight, so my evening is free. Would you like to hang out and watch movies?"

I stare at him.

"Just me and you, hanging out, like friends?" I ask.

He grins again and I'd like to lick his lips.

"Aren't we friends?"

I stare at him again. "I guess so. I hadn't thought of it that way. But I guess we are."

"And don't friends hang out?" Colby reasons. "I'm not Shade right now, I'm Colby."

I nod slowly. "Of course. Colby and Allison can be friends. Shade and Alli Cat can't, because they are client and clientele."

"Now you're getting it," Colby answers, chuckling. "It's how I separate the crazy in my life."

I have to laugh. "I'm going to have to take lessons," I answer. "Because the crazy in my life is getting out of hand."

Colby (not Shade!) takes a seat as I pad into the house, pulling on a shirt as I go. I don't feel the need to have Rick the Dick ogle me again. I still want to bathe in iodine from the first time.

I find Rick strolling down the hallway, away from my bedroom.

"What are you doing?" I ask suspiciously. "You have no need to be in my bedroom."

"Oh, don't I know it," Rick answers with a scowl. "I was hunting for my favorite silver cufflinks- the ones my mother gave to me for my college graduation. They mysteriously vanished when I moved out."

"Did you find them?" I raise an eyebrow. Rick shakes his head.

"No, but I found your little friend."

I'm confused for a second until I see his smug grin.

"You know, you should have said that your 'great sex' that you've been having is with your new dildo." Rick smiles, an evil, disgusting smile. He's so sure that he is God's gift to women. It makes me want to puke.

And then he tosses it to me. Rick was holding Geronimo in his bare hands? I'm going to have to swab it with alcohol before its next use. Or maybe I'll just buy a new one.

"Oh, this," I reply, as nonchalantly as I can while holding a giant dildo in my hand. "This is what I use on the nights when I'm too tired to go out. My new boyfriend wears me out."

Rick stares at me, trying to decide if I'm telling him the truth or not.

"If you really do have a new boyfriend," he says, "Then I need to meet him if he's going to be around

Sophie. That's in our divorce agreement. YOU put that in our divorce agreement."

I smile angelically. Or I hope it is angelically.

"Yes, I did, didn't I? And when I decide that it's time for Sophie to meet him, I'll arrange a meeting with you, as well."

Rick glares at me. "I can't wait to tell your newest victim all about you."

I roll my eyes and start to reply when Sophie comes out from her bedroom. I shove Geronimo behind my back.

"Can you guys stop arguing please?" she demands. "I hate it. I thought it was going to stop when you got divorced."

I instantly feel guilty, particularly given what I'm holding. Mom of the year, right here.

"I'm sorry, Soph," I tell her sincerely. "I didn't know you could hear."

She glances at me. "Of course I can hear. I'm not deaf and you're right outside of my room. And dad, stay out of mom's room. It's not your bedroom anymore. Her dildos are her business, not yours."

I want to freaking die. My cheeks flood with color and Rick glances at me, laughter in his eyes. Sophie didn't mean to make him happy with that remark, but she so, so did. I'm seething inside as Rick makes gestures behind Sophie's back of himself using a dildo. Only, he's pretending to be me, obviously.

So, obviously, I do what any mature women would do. I make a motion that I'm stabbing him in the head with a butcher knife. But in this case, I'm using my dildo.

We both drop our hands when Sophie turns abruptly around. "You know there's a mirror in front of us, right?"

Fuck. She's right. I should definitely know, since I'm the one who hung it at the end of the hall.

Mom of the year, right freaking here.

She rolls her eyes and turns around, dragging her over-night bag behind her. In the kitchen, she turns and kisses my cheek.

"Are you going to be alright?" she asks. I am surprised by her moment of thinking outside of herself. Teenagers are, as a whole, self-absorbed monsters. I smile at her.

"I'll be fine," I tell her. "Really. Your dad and I are fine. We just argue from time to time."

And pretend to kill each other in mime.

With dildos.

That's normal, right?

She shakes her head again. "Okay. I'll be home tomorrow. I have my cell if you need me."

"I'm fine, honey," I insist. "Honestly."

She smiles and leaves with her father, who doesn't say another word. I can't believe that Sophie is concerned for me. Is my little monster growing up into a compassionate human being?

I am smiling to myself at that thought when I remember Shade. Colby. Crap.

I drop Geronimo back into my room and then hurry back out to the patio to find him settled into a lounger, scrolling through his phone.

"Hi," he grins. "Everything okay?"

I smile back.

"Everything is fine. Want to go in the house? Should we go out and eat or should we order in... or?"

He shrugs. "Whatever you were planning to do."

I was going to order takeout, eat every bit of it, watch a chick-flick so that I can cry my guts out in order to stabilize my emotional health and then probably use the services of Geronimo.

But I don't say that.

"I was just going to get Chinese," I tell him. "And then eat it in front of the TV."

"Sounds like heaven," he tells me. "You know what? There's an old horror movie marathon on tonight."

I raise an eyebrow. "Are you trying to say we should watch it because I'm old and so I'll feel right at home?"

He looks appalled. "No, of course not! I---"

I interrupt. "I'm kidding, obviously." I laugh. "I'm not old. I'm in my sexual prime, remember?" I smile. "Old horror movies? You like those?"

He nods. "My dad and I used to stay up late and watch them when I was little. It's a good memory that I have."

"And you don't have any good memories of him now?"

For some reason, it sounded like that is what he meant. He shrugs.

"My dad and I just don't see eye to eye right now. He wants me to do things that I don't want to do. But I'm not exactly sure what I want to do, so that's the problem."

"Does he know about this?" I gesture toward him, but he knows what I mean.

"He doesn't know about Shade. Hell no. No one in my family does."

I nod as I open the patio door and we walk in.

"That must get stressful."

I pour us each a drink.

"Not so much," Colby answers. "I just keep my life compartmentalized. It's pretty easy."

"Again, can you give me lessons?" I ask with a small laugh. Shade laughs too.

"I already gave you a lesson last night," he answers. "Isn't one lesson a week enough?"

Memories from last night flood through me and weaken my knees. And I have to agree.

"You're right. This pupil is ready for a rest. Come on-I'll show you to the media room."

"I like the sound of that," Colby answers as he pulls on his shirt. He sounds tired.

I show him the way and then run back upstairs to throw on a pair of sweats and a t-shirt. Hey, don't judge. He told me to do what I would've done if he weren't here. My plans definitely involved my favorite sweatpants.

And so, that is how our night begins. With me in sweats curled up next to Colby under a warm blanket. My media room is always chilly, so I always keep fuzzy blankets available and tonight, it certainly comes in handy.

We pop popcorn and share each other's Chinese. We then watch goofy old movies until Colby decides that I need to learn to make jello shots, because they are apparently delicious and a necessity in life. So we run up to the kitchen and mix up a batch, leaving them in the fridge to set up while we watch another movie.

After the stupidest and corniest horror movie in the history of the earth is finally over, we return to the kitchen to try our handiwork.

Colby hands me a cherry one, while he takes a lime.

"Why did you have these little cups on hand, anyway?" he asks me as he pops the lid off.

"Honestly, I don't remember," I tell him. "I think Sophie needed them for a fundraiser that she was doing for her cheerleading squad last year."

"Well, here's to cheerleading then," Colby toasts with his little plastic cup. And then he scoops the jello out with his tongue. I do the same.

I nod, processing the flavor. "I can barely taste the vodka," I tell him. He nods back.

"That's the point," he says. He hands me another. "That's why they go down so smoothly."

We again scoop the jello out with our tongues. I can't help but watch Colby's tongue. I know personally that it is a very skilled tongue. But tonight, he is Colby. *And things are different when he is Colby*, I remind myself. *And I should probably be concerned that I'm spending my Saturday night hanging out with a young gigolo.*

But apparently, jello shots have a way of sneaking up on you and changing the way you previously thought of something.

Because as Colby and I laugh and joke, we manage to do several (as in ten) more jello shots each. And then one of us (me) decides that we should do body-shots because I've never done one.

"Seriously, I tell him. "Can you show me how? Because I think it's a life skill that one ought to have."

I'm drunk. And I'm a big enough person to say that I'm drunk.

"I'm drunk," I add. "And that's definitely a good time to learn to do a body shot."

Colby looks at me, studying me. He's oh-so-handsome. And it's easy to forget, in this moment, that he is younger than me. And that I should only think of him this way when he's Shade. Because damn, he's sexy. I take a deep breath.

Colby smiles. "You're right. A body shot is a life skill that you should definitely master. Come on- I'll do one on you to demonstrate and then you can do one on me. Do you have tequila?"

I nod, suddenly very fascinated by the prospect of this lesson.

"Do you have salt and limes?"

Again, I nod as Colby searches through the kitchen. As he does, I clean off the granite breakfast bar. He turns around with all of the supplies that we need and finds me stripping down.

He raises an eyebrow.

"I don't want to get tequila on my favorite sweats," I shrug innocently. Which of course doesn't explain why I'm stripping off my panties and bra, too.

I'm so going to hell.

He laughs and helps me onto the bar. I stretch my feet out and put my arms behind my head. The granite is cold beneath me and I shiver.

"Want me to warm you up?" Colby asks, his gaze wicked. He's looking at me with a Shade-like stare and I shiver again.

Then nod.

I'm shameless.

I have no shame.

I'm going to hell.

I am chanting these things silently in my head. And when Colby strips off his shirt, I stop chanting. I can't help it. The guy is gorgeous. And distracting.

He shrugs. "I don't want to get tequila on my favorite t-shirt."

Warmth instantly floods my nether-region as he presses against my side. His skin is warm and firm.

He cuts a lime wedge and places it between my teeth. Then he shakes some salt around my breasts, concentrating quite a lot on my nipples. And then he pours tequila into my navel. I silently thank God that I am a very meticulous belly-button washer.

My breakfast bar is the perfect height for this activity-I'm right in front of Colby's chest. He has easy access to every part of me that he needs.

He bends and starts at my ankle, kissing and sucking and licking his way upward. When he gets to my thigh, he pays special attention, suckling very intently. Chills run up my body and fire shoots into BB. Because BB is a shameless hussy, she wants this even more than I do. And then he drags his tongue deliberately and teasingly over her.

My legs straighten out like boards as my heart starts to race.

He licks his way to my belly button, by-passing it and concentrating instead on my breasts. He sucks every bit of salt off of each one, tantalizing me by licking, sucking and nipping at my nipples. I am literally arching against him before he is done, but he holds me down.

"You'll spill your tequila," he whispers into my ear. His breath is hot against my skin.

I grip the side of the breakfast bar. I seriously do have amazing fortitude. Otherwise, I'd have abandoned this activity, leaped off this granite slap and straddled this man-boy on my kitchen floor.

But as it is, I remain still.

With a lime wedge between my teeth.

Colby makes his way down to my belly-button and as he does, his right hand finds BB. He laps at the tequila while his hand makes lazy circles around BB... and then he slides a finger into her.

I almost come off of the table.

Amazing fortitude, I chant.

Amazing fucking fortitude.

Colby drinks every drop of tequila and then slides over me back up to my mouth. His dark eyes meet mine and I am dying to feel his lips on my own... his full, luscious lips.

Finally, finally, his lips touch mine as he takes the lime wedge without using his hands. He sucks on it and then spits it to the side. I know that my housekeeper is going to want a raise tomorrow. But I don't care tonight.

Tonight, I pull Colby's face to mine and I inhale his kiss. I kiss him so hard and so long that I can't see straight. I can't think straight. I am no longer bound by logic or reason or rules. I don't care what his name is right now, Colby or Shade or even Cat in the Freaking Hat. I only want him inside of me.

He slides me off of the bar and lays me on the floor.
There is a brief rustle of foil and then I get my wish.

Chapter Fourteen

(Or: It's all fun and games until you wake up naked)

We wake up in the light of day in my bed. I don't remember making it to the bedroom at any point and quite possibly, Colby carried me here.

I lean up on my elbow and study him. He's sleeping and he looks so young while he's asleep.

Because he is *young,* my mind reminds me devilishly. *He's almost young enough to be your kid.*

No, he's not! The other half of my brain argues. *Not even close.*

Great.

I sigh. Now I'm arguing with myself. I'm pretty sure that's a sign of insanity. All I need to do now is start rocking in my seat and begin mumbling and Sophie can get me committed.

Sophie!

I glance at the clock and sigh a breath of relief. It's only 10:00 am. She won't be home for a few hours.

"Good morning," Colby says, stretching beside me.

I look over at him again. He's adorably cute when he just wakes up. His hair is tousled and his eyes are glassy with sleep.

"I'm sorry," I tell him. "Did I wake you?"

He shakes his head. "Nope. I've been awake. I was just lying here with my eyes closed listening to you snore."

"I don't snore!" I protest with a giggle. "I don't."

"Oh, you do," he insists, leaning over to kiss me. "But it's cute."

His kiss is soft and gentle. And scary.

We shouldn't be kissing or naked right now in the light of day. Or in bed together naked. And kissing. He's Colby and I'm Allison. He's way younger than me. And this isn't cool.

I draw back.

"Is everything alright?" his eyebrows knit together. I shake my head.

"I don't know. We shouldn't have done that. You're Colby right now. And I'm Allison. And this isn't something we should be doing."

Colby is still for a moment, then sits up. I have to ignore the way his abs flex when he moves if I want to continue any kind of cognitive thought.

"You're right," he agrees. "We got carried away. It happens. It tends to happen a lot when body shots are involved," he adds wryly. He turns to me.

"But it's not the end of the world, Alli. It was a slip. No big deal. It was fun. We're friends. And last night, we were friends with benefits. Don't freak out, okay?"

Don't freak out. What a young thing to say. I am reminded for the fourteenth time today already how young he is. I nod.

"Okay."

Colby swings his leg over the side of the bed and stands up. I can't help but look. I've got amazing fortitude, but I'm not a freaking nun. And then I wish I hadn't looked. He's standing there in the sunlight in all of his twenty-two (or twenty three?) year old perfection and I immediately want him to come back to bed. But I swallow hard and suppress that thought.

Get thee back to hell, Satan, where you belong! I silently chastise my thoughts.

"Since I'm here now, though, do you want to take a shower with me?" Colby asks impishly. He turns and I see the full profile of his body now, semi-erect member and all. Mother Nature at her finest. I decide that she very probably is a woman, after all. She made men like Colby as gifts to the female species.

I nod, against the will of my logical thoughts. "Yes."

He hauls me to my feet and drags me to my shower.

Apparently, Satan didn't get himself back into hell, like I demanded. He controlled my thoughts in the shower instead, because Colby and I have sex in every conceivable position known to man in there... along with a few more that Satan invented on the fly.

When the mirrors are all fogged and we are completely spent and finished, we stumble out into the cold air.

"Well," I sigh wryly. "I won't need to go to Yoga this week."

Colby laughs and towels off.

"I like you, Alli. For real. And not just because you pay me to."

My heart stops. I think. His expression right now is so sweet, but this isn't what I want. I can't 'date' a twenty-something. I can't have a real relationship of any kind with him…not even a friends-with-benefits arrangement. I look at him and he immediately sees it on my face and he backpedals.

"I didn't mean… I meant…" He is stammering now and it's the first time that I have seen him in any way other than cool and collected. For once, he seems like the twenty-two (or twenty-three!) year old that he actually is.

"It's okay," I say, interrupting him. "I don't know where you were going with that, but it's fine. I'm just not ready for a relationship yet. You're amazing and awesome and I like you, too, though."

"That's what I meant to say," he says and I can't tell by his face if that is the truth or not. "I only meant to say that I like you. That you're awesome and I consider you my friend."

I smile, warm rushing through me.

"I consider you my friend, too. This is one idea that Sara had that was actually a good one."

"So I was Sara's idea?" Colby asks with a grin as he pulls on his clothes.

I nod. "Who else's?"

He laughs. "Good point. That friend of yours is something else."

"That she is," I agree. "She gets me into all kinds of trouble. But this particular trouble… well, I like it. But I like it how it is now. I don't want it to change."

Meaning, I'm not going to date a twenty-something kid. Even if he is sexy as hell and taught me how to bring a man to his knees in five minutes flat.

He smiles at me. "Message received, Alli Cat. We can be friends, though. And you're still my client, right?"

I nod. "Of course."

Because I want to lick your body too much to cancel that, I add silently.

"Good," he says. "Now, I'm gonna get going. Do you want me to get you a coffee or something before I go?"

I shake my head. "No, I'm getting up."

He bends and kisses my forehead. "Last night was fun. Call and set up an appointment for next weekend, okay?" I nod again.

And then he's gone.

And I'm alone in my room.

I throw on my robe and pad down to the kitchen to make some coffee. I eye the damage. There is salt sprinkled on the floor, my clothes are in the middle of the room and everything is cleared off the breakfast bar.

I smile at the memory of last night.

Well, no one can say that I'm not daring and fun.

I sigh and start to clean up the carnage.

****

"You did what??" Sara is astonished and practically speechless, which is something that I feel compelled to mark on my calendar. "You spent the night with him in your house?"

I nod. "Yup. And he was Colby, not Shade. I've clearly blurred some sort of invisible boundary. But I cleared it up with him. It was a temporary slip. Things will go back to normal now."

Sara eyes me doubtfully. We are in the middle of the park again for lunch and so she has to keep her voice down or she will scare the little old folks who come here to feed the ducks.

"I don't know about that," she says. "I think it's one of those situations where once you cross that line nothing will ever be the same. I mean, you've had sex with Colby now. Before, you just had sex with Shade. This is huge, Alli. Maybe you should just consider dating him."

I stare at her.

But not before those images flash through my head. Me and Colby, dating. Going to the movies. Having dinner. Having people mistake him for my son. No, thank you.

So I tell her that.

"People would think he's my son," I say firmly. "And while I like the arrangement that we have, I'm not going to date him. Not gonna happen, Sara."

She clamps her mouth shut. "We'll see, Miss Tightly Wound. We'll see."

"No, we won't," I tell her. "Not this time. But speaking of seeing... Look at my face and tell me what you see."

I lean over my turkey club and shove my face into hers. She's startled for a second, but then she peers into mine, her eyes staring into my own.

"What exactly am I looking for?" she asks as she examines me.

"My crow's feet," I answer. "How bad are they? Rick the Dick was at my house this weekend and among other things, he mentioned that I have horrible crow's feet. Do I?"

She turns my face to and fro in the light.

"They're there," she announces. "But they're not horrible. Rick is a dick. Obviously. You're thirty-five. You're going to have laugh lines. We laugh a lot. It's unavoidable."

Sara picks her sandwich back up and chomps on it, unconcerned.

"Is it?" I answer thoughtfully, staring into space. "Have you ever tried Botox?"

Sara almost chokes and I whomp her on her back. I briefly remember the Brazilian wax incident and whomp a little harder than necessary. Then I smile evilly. Whomping her thin little back is surprisingly satisfying.

"Are you serious?" she chokes out, wiping her mouth on a napkin as she shoves my hand away. "You're not getting Botox. You know what that is, right? It's the bacteria that causes botulism. It's a freaking toxin."

"Oh, I know," I tell her. "And I'm not getting Botox. *We* are."

She chokes again.

"No. If you think that... no." She stares at me as firmly as she can, looking down her skinny nose at me. Her short, spiky red hair looks like even it has risen up in mutiny against me, as well. I smile.

"Oh, yes," I tell her. "I dated a gigolo, had sex with the gigolo, bought a sex toy and had a Brazilian wax. All at your behest. And I have to admit, those were good ideas. You're going to have to concede that sometimes I have good ideas too. I'm pretty sure that this is one of those times."

She is stammering now. Utterly speechless. I'm definitely going to have to mark this on the calendar.

"But... but... botulism is a bacteria. Injected *into my face*! That's different than..."

"Different than a stranger's penis injected into my vagina?" I ask innocently. Sara all but sputters.

"No, but you liked it!"

"Of course I liked it!" I stare at her like she's grown two heads. "That penis is attached to a perfect twenty-something body. And I'm sure that you will like the Botox, as well. You've got crow's feet too, you know. I've never wanted to say anything before. But you might as well know. We could both use an age-eraser. And that's exactly what Botox is. And supposedly, it doesn't even hurt."

"You're the devil," Sara announces as she cleans up her lunch trash.

"Irrelevant," I answer sweetly, throwing her words from the other day back at her. "And you're a devil, too. That's why we love each other so much. I'll make the appointment."

"I can't do it tonight," she snaps. "I have Spinning."

"That's fine," I say soothingly. "I'm sure they have openings for tomorrow night."

Sara flounces off, but not before glaring at me a couple of times for good measure. She turns and flips me off with both hands when she's halfway to her car. Both hands—because she means business. I laugh and the elderly lady sitting next to us gasps.

I lean over. "I'm sorry about that, m'am."

But I'm really not. It feels good to get one over on Sara for once in my life. It's been a long time coming. She's usually the one pulling this kind of shit.

I'm in a fabulous mood as I return to my office and enlist Taylor's help in researching the best plastic surgeon in town with Botox. She's got an appointment for Sara and I within the hour.

"What are you smiling about?" Alex asks as he breezes into my office.

I turn away from my computer and smile at my new boss. There's no way I'm going to tell him that I'm laughing because I just emailed Sara the time of our Botox appointment for tomorrow night. I can practically hear her screaming from here and that gives me great joy. I might be somewhat sadistic and I can't have my new boss knowing that.

"Nothing in particular," I tell him. "I'm just in a good mood, I guess."

"On a Monday?" Alex raises one handsome eyebrow. Yes, even his eyebrows are sexy. I smile.

"I guess so. I know. I must be an alien or something."

"I think you must surely be an alien."

Alex smiles again and once again, I have the strangest feeling that I know him. But once again, I know that I don't. I would remember such a sexy face. And body. Of that, I am certain. I absently wonder how many hours a week he spends in the gym.

"I've got our meeting nailed down with the supplier," he tells me, bringing my thoughts back to the present. "Can you be ready to leave by Thursday evening? The meeting is Friday morning in San Diego. We'll do the meeting and then fly back that evening."

I glance at my calendar. I can surely have Sophie stay Thursday night with Rick. And if not, Sara will take her.

"Of course," I tell him. "That'll be fine. I'll be ready."

"Great," he answers. "I'll have Libby email the details to Taylor. And I've brought you the background info on their company so that you're up to speed." He hands me the file.

"Perfect," I smile.

I expect him to leave, but he doesn't. He lingers, chatting about little things…this and that. I find myself watching him. The way he moves, the easy way he speaks.

Alex is definitely handsome in a very grown up way. Refined and gorgeous. He's obviously grown comfortable in his skin and he wears it well. His suits are expensive and tailored, his shoes are perfectly polished. His smile is…well, intoxicating. I know it sounds corny to say, but it's true. And he's smiling at me right now.

"So, what do you think? Is it doable?"

Doable? Hell yes, he's doable. But wait.

Uh-oh. He asked me for something and I have no idea what.

"Um, sure," I answer.

Please Lord, don't let me be agreeing to something horrible, I silently pray.

Although, I'm not sure God will be that inclined to help since I only don't know what Alex said because I had been pondering how sexy he is.

Alex grins, the warmth spreading to his deep blue eyes.

"Perfect! I'll have Libby take care of the intern paperwork and I'll tell my son he can start when we return from our trip. Thank you, Alli. I appreciate this."

I freeze. Intern?

Craaaaaaap. Why wasn't I paying attention? I don't have time for an intern. But I can hardly say no now.

Instead, I smile. "Of course. It's not a problem. We can surely find something for him to do."

Alex unfolds from the chair and grins one more time, then he's gone.

I drop my head to my desk.

I'm such an idiot.

I reluctantly pick my head up so that I can e-mail Taylor the good news. She's in charge of another intern. And not just any intern, but the son of our senior VP. She's going to kill me.

I hear her shriek when she reads it, so I run to my door and lock it so that she can't commit any form of physical violence upon me. I'm too young to die.

****

"I'm going to kill you," Sara tells me. And from the look on her face as we walk up to the plastic surgeon's office, she might mean it. I take a step away from her to be on the safe side.

"It's going to be fine," I assure her.

Although to be honest, I'm not feeling that confident. I'd always said that I'd never get plastic surgery of any sort. And even though an injection of botulism to the face isn't exactly surgery, it isn't exactly making me feel all warm and fuzzy, either.

"People do this all the time," I continue, as we check in and sit in the posh waiting room. A water wall flows to our left and my feet are resting on a teak floor. "And this guy must be really good. Check out this waiting room! They even have chocolate."

I motion to the little café area on the side, where there is a mocha/coffee/latte machine and baskets of chocolate bars.

Sara rolls her eyes. "Hmph. He's just trying to create repeat customers. He wants to bring us back for liposuction."

I chuckle and pick up a magazine. But I don't have to wait long enough for me to read it. They call us and we go back together, led by a very trim Barbie-esque nurse.

After having our faces poked with long needles for a brief moment, we are walking back out within minutes.

It was quick, it was painless, and it was nothing like the experience-from-hell that I had with the Brazilian wax. It almost doesn't seem fair—it seems like there should have been some pain involved to pay Sara back. I turn to her.

"See? We're fine. And within a couple of days, we're going to look ten years younger. You can thank me then, if you like. You don't need to do it now."

I laugh and she glares.

But that entire scenario is reversed in the morning.

****

When Sara stops by my house to check out my face, she laughs until she almost pees her pants. Because I look like the Elephant Man. Or, rather, I look like the Elephant Man would've looked if he had just had an allergic reaction to botulism.

I am wailing as Sara laughs when Sophie bursts into my bathroom.

I see my daughter visibly flinch as she looks at my face. And to be fair, it looks like my face has been hit with a garbage truck.

My eyes are swollen to the point where I am basically peering out from two puffy dough piles with slits in them. There are faint shadows under my eyes and I'm not certain, but I think there is even a broken blood vessel in my left eye. I can't tell though, because I can't open it far enough to examine it.

"Oh, my god! Who did this to you?" Sophie demands, rushing to me and spinning me around. "I swear to god, if Dad did this, I'm going to kill him. We'll call the police."

I stare at her for a minute in confusion, before I realize that she thinks someone beat me up. I look so bad that it looks like someone punched my face in.

Sara is dying now.

Sophie glares at her. "How can you laugh like that? I think my mom needs a doctor."

Sara howls.

"Your mom already saw a doctor," she gasps. "That's what happened. It's called Botox, sweetie. And your mom insisted that we go. And apparently, because of a little thing called Karma, your mom has had some sort of reaction."

Sara is picking up her cell phone as she speaks, punching in a number. A minute later, she's talking to the doctor's office. She nods and agrees with someone and then turns to me.

"Are you having problems breathing?"

Sophie gasps and I shake my head quickly.

"No."

Sara relays that to the nurse, then nods again before hanging up.

"Yep. It sounds like you had a reaction. She said that the swelling should wear off within a day or two probably. If you have difficulty breathing or swallowing, you're supposed to go to the emergency room. Otherwise, you can use over the counter meds for the discomfort and ice packs. I'm so glad that we did this, aren't you? What a great idea this was."

She raises a sarcastic red eyebrow at me. And I glare at her.

"I can't go anywhere," I growl. "Not looking like this. I look like I belong in a women's shelter."

Sara finally takes pity on me and stops laughing. She actually hugs my shoulders a little.

"I think this has taught us a valuable lesson," she says seriously.

I nod. "To never have a toxin inserted into our faces?"

She nods. "That, but also, this is why we leave decisions like this to me. I'm the one with the brilliant ideas."

I don't bother rolling my eyes because no one would be able to tell anyway. Instead, I just stomp to my bed and drop into it, covering up my head.

Sophie brings me an ice pack when she leaves for school because clearly she is an angel. She gets that trait from her mother. I thank her and give her $20 for lunch. I press the ice to my poor face and pick up the remote. If I'm going to be in bed, I'm going to use it to my full advantage and watch the Lifetime channel all day.

And that is exactly what I do. That is, until my cell phone rings at 4:00 pm. I see from the ID that it is the office, so I have to answer.

It's Taylor.

"Hey boss," she greets me cheerfully. "Are you feeling better?"

I had called in this morning and said that I had the flu. Obviously, there was no way that I could tell them the truth.

"A little," I answer truthfully. "Hopefully, I'll be back in tomorrow."

"Good deal," she replies. "Hey, I'm calling because Alex came by and asked me for the file that he gave you yesterday—the one with the background info on the supplier that you're going to see this week? I told him that you have it in your briefcase. That's right, isn't it?"

I nod, then remember that she can't see me.

"Yes, I have it in my bag. I'll give it to him tomorrow."

"Well, that's the thing." And I freeze at her hesitant tone. Taylor is never, ever hesitant. It's part of her charm.

"What's the thing?" I ask nervously.

"He needs it today because he's putting together some sort of report or brief or something for the meeting. He had to leave early for an appointment and he wanted your address so he could swing by and pick it up afterward. I gave it to him- I didn't figure you'd mind."

I want to kill myself. Seriously. Clearly, suicide is the only way out of this.

"When is he leaving, do you know?" I'm surprised that I am able to ask this calmly. I can see a vague reflection of myself in the TV screen and it isn't pretty.

"He left over an hour ago. I'm guessing that he should be there any time."

I grit my teeth and take a breath. A very fast breath, since I don't have a lot of time.

"Taylor, I need you to add something to my calendar for tomorrow morning."

"Okay- I've got it pulled up. I'm ready," she says. "What is it?"

"Put, 'Kill Taylor' in a one-hour block of time at 9:00 am. I want to have plenty of time."

I then hang up for emphasis.

I'll apologize tomorrow. For now, I've got to figure out what to do.

I briefly consider wearing a Muslim hijab and only shoot the idea down because I don't have one on hand.

As I'm flying around the room, on the very verge of hysteria, I remember the cooling gel mask that came in a spa kit that Sophie gave me for Christmas. It's in the freezer right now, probably buried under thirty-four bags of frozen peas. I've never used it. And I never make frozen peas, either.

I make a run for the fridge.

I'll look ridiculous, but it's better than looking like the Elephant Man.

As I dig through all of the frozen food in my freezer, I am starting to panic because I can't find it right when I hear a car door slam closed in my driveway.

Craaaaaap.

And then, a miracle. I find the mask buried in the back.

"Thank you, God," I whisper.

My heart thunders in my chest as I slide the mask over my head and situate it on my face. I don't even have time to look in the mirror. I can only pray that it hides my hideousness.

The doorbell rings and I straighten my night-shirt and stick my shoulders back. The only way to carry this off is to be confident. And act normally. Everyone answers the door in pajamas and a spa mask, right?

I stride for the door.

I know that I look ridiculous, but I don't care. And besides, it can't be helped, anyway.

I throw the door open.

And Alex flinches in the same exact way that Sophie did.

I seriously want to die.

Chapter Fifteen

(Because now is a perfect time to hear from Alex)

Alex

"Holy shit," I say, before I can help it.

I'm staring at Allison and she looks like a semi has plowed into her. Into her face, specifically. She also looks like she is attending some strange sort of masquerade ball as a disheveled, abused housewife. She's wearing a night-shirt, bare feet, messy hair and some sort of ice mask. If I weren't instantly concerned about her well-being, I would laugh.

"Were you attacked?" I ask as I step inside. Alli looks like she wants to either hit me or curl up in a corner. I can't tell which.

She shakes her head. "No." And then she sighs.

"Are you alright?" I ask, examining her again. She's got bruising along her cheekbones. "Did someone hurt you?"

She flushes, or at least, I think she flushes. It's hard to tell from behind the mask.

This is a side to Alli that I haven't seen yet. Usually, she is fierce and strong—a true dynamo. To be honest, when I first met her, I was a little intimidated. The woman certainly has game. And she's beautiful, which makes her a force to be reckoned with.

And by now, I'm seeing that nothing else appears to be wrong with her. No other marks on her other than her face.

And she's shaking her head.

"No, no one hurt me. Except for a doctor. But I paid him to because I'm an idiot."

I raise an eyebrow because now I'm confused.

"What?"

She is sighing again and she looks embarrassed. Or she appears to be, from behind her ice mask. I stare at her, waiting for her to explain.

She lifts a slender shoulder, shrugging.

"I had Botox. And then I had a bad reaction to the Botox."

I can't help it. I laugh.

And even the indignant and embarrassed expression on Alli's normally lovely face doesn't keep me from laughing harder and harder. I literally have tears pouring down my cheeks before I am finally able to control myself.

"I'm glad I can amuse you," Allis says. From what I can tell, her cheekbones are blushing even more now. Her very swollen cheekbones.

I swallow what is left of my amusement.

"Are you in pain?" I ask. She shakes her head.

"No. I just look like hell. Won't you come in?" She gestures with her arm and I step further into her house.

Her home is beautiful, exactly like I expected. Expensive furnishings, tasteful art, a lot of natural light and modern conveniences. She leads me to the kitchen, where she digs through her bag.

"You didn't need Botox," I tell her stiff spine. I clearly put her on the defensive by laughing and I didn't mean to. "You look great. I'm sorry for laughing. I was laughing because the idea that you would do that when you look great already just shocked me."

And her spine loosens.

Sometimes, I guess I can pull it out and say something tactful. I've learned something in forty years, apparently.

She turns, a small smile on her lips.

"Thank you," she says graciously, handing me the file. "And I don't blame you for laughing. My best friend laughed too."

"Nice best friend," I answer. Alli smiles again.

"Well, to be fair, I talked her into having it done with me and so she thought it was fitting. Karma and all. But she's talked me into a hundred different things...all of them worse than this, I can assure you."

I stare at her. "Worse than Botox?" I am doubtful.

She nods. "Oh, yes. Far worse. But they're a little inappropriate to discuss with my boss."

And now I'm intrigued. But obviously, I can't ask. She's already standing in front of me in a night-shirt. To talk about inappropriate things at the same time would be over-the-line, probably.

Particularly since I'm attracted to her. I'd admitted that to myself the first time we'd met. After I got over being intimidated, that is. Hey, she's a gorgeous, smart woman and I'm a red-blooded male. It's only normal.

I take a step toward her.

"What did they tell you to do for it? When do you think the swelling will go down?"

"I'm taking ibuprofen and using an ice pack," she says, tugging the mask down a little. I think on that.

"Shouldn't you be using an antihistamine cream? My sister gets hives sometimes and she uses a cream to take down the swelling. Do you have any?"

"Ooh- that's a great idea!" Alli exclaims, turning around immediately. "I keep some on hand for my daughter, Sophie. She actually gets hives sometimes, too! Thank you for reminding me!" she calls over her shoulder as she starts down a hallway. "I'll be right back."

"Take your time!" I answer.

I sit down at a breakfast bar stool and wait, looking around as I do. Stainless steel appliances, granite counters, spotless surroundings. I'm not sure if she actually uses her kitchen, but it sure is nice. A plate of fresh lemons and limes sit next to me. Among the various art hanging on the wall, there is a picture of a smiling teenage girl. Hazel eyes, gorgeous smile, dark hair. The girl looks just like Alli- it has to be her daughter.

As I'm looking at it, my phone rings.

I glance at it. My son's number flashes on the screen.

I sigh and pick it up.

"Hey, Colby."

"Hi dad," my son answers coolly. "I got your message. I don't really want to do an internship at your new job. I've told you this a hundred times before."

"Really?" I answer, as patiently as I can. "What else are you going to do? You've got a college degree. You've got to figure things out and decide what you're going to do. You're twenty-three years old."

"So you've said…many times before," Colby answers. I fight really hard to bite out a sarcastic come-back. My son is head-strong, a trait that he might get from me. Or he definitely does, according to my ex-wife.

"Look, you can start on Monday. The pay is decent and you'll get your foot in the door of a really great company to work for. You are a creative person and I think you'll see that marketing is a great fit for your imaginative mind. Come to Zellers' headquarters on Monday and ask for Allison Lancaster at the front desk. She's the executive director in charge of marketing. She reports to me and I think you'll like her."

Colby is silent for a second before he responds.

"Allison Lancaster, huh? Okay. I'll ask for her on Monday and I'll give it a shot. You obviously feel strongly about it."

I am stunned but I try hard not to show it. "Excellent! I'm glad you've changed your mind. I'm certain this is the right decision, Colby."

"Well, we'll see," he responds.

We hang up and I exhale slowly.

My son is certainly full of surprises.

As is my new executive director. I turn in my seat, waiting for her to re-emerge from the hall. My son is as stubborn and headstrong as I can be. I hope Alli can manage him.

Chapter Sixteen

(Because obviously we have to hear from Colby at this point)

Colby

Holy shit!

I hang up my phone and sit in stunned silence in my bedroom.

Allison Lancaster works for my father. And I will be working for her on Monday. In a non-sexual capacity, I mean. She's going to die. She's going to fucking die. I can practically see the expression on her face right now.

I glance at my phone. I should call her and give her a head's up. But then hesitate.

A devilish idea comes to mind and I can't help but smile. Allison is adorable when she's embarrassed. I remember the look on her face in the restaurant when she was trying not to orgasm in front of the waiter. And then the crotch of my pants shrinks two sizes at the memory of what followed after that…in the restaurant's bathroom.

So instead, I pick up my phone and text her.

Why don't you make an appointment with me on Saturday? I need my Alli Cat fix.

I set my phone down.

I'm not going to tell her. I'll surprise her when I show up on Monday. The look on her face will be worth it.

Chapter Seventeen

(Or: Lines are made to be crossed, aren't they?)

Alli

I have just slathered on antihistamine cream while staring in the bathroom mirror when my phone buzzes with a text. I wipe my hands off and pick it up.

Shade.

Why don't you make an appointment with me on Saturday? I need my Alli Cat fix.

I can't help but smile.

I'm so glad that I drew the line in the sand with him—and made sure that he knows that I can never date him. But that doesn't mean that I'm ever going to stop using his services. And then I feel ultra-naughty for thinking that, considering my new boss is waiting for me in my kitchen. My ultra-sexy-I-might-even-have-a-crush-on new boss. The very one.

I answer Shade: *I'll think about it.*

But I know that I will. I'll get home from San Diego on Friday evening, so I can probably even do it that night. Or I can play it safe and make the appointment for Saturday. We'll see.

I apply some concealer beneath my cheeks and then pick up my jar of bronzer powder. I apply some with the brush, then examine myself in the mirror. The swelling is still there, but at least the bruising is concealed. I still look like I went five rounds in the boxing ring with a prize fighter, though.

I look at myself again. Make that ten rounds.

At that moment, I hear Alex calling me.

"Can I grab a drink from your fridge?"

I start to answer, but realize that he wouldn't be able to hear me. I walk back out to the kitchen and try to ignore the fact that he can see my Elephant Man face more clearly now that the mask is gone.

"Of course," I tell him, walking to the fridge. "What would you like?"

Alex slides off the stool and circles the breakfast bar, quickly coming to my side.

"You didn't have to come out and get it," he tells me, reaching for the fridge handle at the same time as I do. "I can do it."

And somehow, and I'll never know exactly how, the jar of bronzing powder flies out of my other hand and explodes in a puff of rust-colored brown dust on the crotch of Alex's very expensive slacks.

On the crotch.

I stare at him in horror and start to stammer.

"I…I'm… so sorry! Oh, my gosh—we should…" He's brushing at it and I grab his arm. "No, don't do that. You'll grind it in. We should…I'll suck it off!" I start to run for the broom-closet but as soon as I realize what I just said, I want to die.

And then I'm frozen.

I'll suck it off???

I turn slowly and meet his amused cobalt gaze.

"I meant, with the vacuum. I'll suck it off with the vacuum hose."

Alex grins, a mischievous grin that lights up his sexier-than-hell face.

"Clearly," he answers. "Whatever else *could* you have meant?"

And I want to die again.

My cheeks are bright red as I yank the vacuum out of the closet, plug it in and then approach him. He grins and holds his hand out.

"I think I should probably do this part," he suggests. "Not that I don't trust you, but…"

And I want to die for a third time.

I hand him the hose with limp fingers and then turn on the vacuum for him, watching him hose off his crotch. This might be the single most awkward situation in the history of my life. Seriously. Or maybe even in anyone's life or in all lives put together.

When he's finished, you can still see faint traces of the bronzer on his gray pants. I sigh.

"I'll pay to have them cleaned, obviously," I tell him. "And if it stains, I'll buy you a new pair."

Alex waves his hand.

"Don't worry about it," he tells me good-naturedly. "Seriously. I showed up here on your sick day unannounced. I deserved it."

He laughs and I can't help but laugh with him.

What a day.

"It seems that the deck is stacked against our having a normal relationship, doesn't it?" Alex chuckles. And at the word relationship, I suck in breath. Can he tell that I've been thinking of him in a very un-boss like way? I swallow.

"I know and that's my fault," I say uncertainly. "I'm really sorry. I promise, I'm usually very professional."

Alex shakes his head. "I wouldn't change you a bit," he announces.

He's so handsome with the evening sun shining on him through the window. I try not to notice it.

"You make going to work interesting," he adds.

"Glad I can be of service," I mumble. "Would you actually like that drink now or should I find something else to dump on you?"

He laughs. "You know, as tempting as that sounds, I should probably get going. I want to look through this file tonight and make some notes. You have a good night, though, and I'll see you tomorrow. I hope your swelling goes down. Honestly, it looks better already. That cream must be helping!"

I touch my cheeks gingerly. He's right. The skin is much more relaxed than it was a bit ago.

"You're right- and thank you for the idea. I hadn't even though of it. Maybe you should have been a doctor."

"Ah, but then I would have had to see naked women all day at work, you know- without their underwear and stuff. Oh, wait! That happens to me now!" He laughs as he watches my face. My face, obviously, explodes into flame.

"I'm kidding," he tells me. "I shouldn't find it so funny, but I can't help it. I hope you don't find it inappropriate. You have to admit that this entire situation is hilarious."

I nod miserably.

"I know. It is," I admit. "Lately, with every stupid stunt that I pull, it feels like I'm having an out of body experience. Like I keep watching someone else do all the dumb stuff that I keep doing."

Alex just chuckles. "Don't worry about it. I had a period after my divorce when I went a little crazy too. It will pass and things will get back to normal again."

I nod because I know he's right, but the trouble is that I don't even know what normal is. I'm going to have to find a new normal, I think. I walk him to the door and thank him for coming to get the file and apologize once again for ruining his crotch.

"Of your pants," I add, stammering.

He grins.

"It was good to see you today, Alli," he smiles. "Really."

And he's gone.

And I've only made it to my hallway before he's back, grinning sheepishly as he pokes his head in the door.

"Um, my car won't start," he says with a shake of his head. "I'm going to call a tow-truck. Then do you mind if I wait here with you?"

I stare at him. "Your car won't start? What in the world do you drive?"

I walk to the window and glance out onto my drive to see a gleaming black BMW. It's clearly brand new.

"Hmm. Well, even the best things break," I say as I turn around. "Of course you can wait in here. Would you like that drink now?"

Alex nods. "That would be great."

He finds a tow-truck company on his phone and then calls them while I pour him a glass of wine. And then one for myself. I motion to him that I'll be right back and I make my way to my bedroom to get dressed.

I have to force myself not to put on something sexy.

I am startled by that inclination.

I want to look sexy for my boss?

But my boss is drop-dead sexy, I remind myself.

So of course I want to look sexy too. I pull on a pair of yoga pants instead and a t-shirt. It's a snug, v-neck t-shirt, but it's still a t-shirt. And the yoga pants do make my ass look good, but they're still yoga pants. I glance into the mirror. My face looks a little better, but it's still not phenomenal. But at least the Elephant Man look is gone. It definitely didn't suit me.

When I return to the kitchen, Alex is off the phone.

"You look better," he announces, looking for all intents and purposes like a GQ model as he turns away from the windows and smiles at me.

"Well, getting dressed will do that to a person," I answer. When I smile now, my face doesn't feel tight from the swelling. That's got to be a good thing.

"Okay," I say as I gaze around my kitchen. "Pretty much the only things that I have to eat are chocolate, popcorn and a bunch of frozen vegetables. I'm hungry though. Want to call in some Chinese while we wait for the tow-truck? I've got them on speed-dial."

Alex laughs. "I thought your kitchen was too clean to actually be used. I'd love Chinese. I know it's only 5:00, but I skipped lunch today since I had to duck out early."

I shrug as I reach for the phone.

"I'm not that much of a cook," I tell him honestly. "But I can bake a frozen pizza with the best of them. And I'm excellent at dialing the phone."

He laughs again as I order our dinner. I then pour us two more glasses of wine and we settle onto the patio to wait.

"So, how did you decide to come to Zellers?" I ask, making polite small talk. I am purposely ignoring the way his stomach is wash-board flat. The only ripples on it are from muscles. And I can practically see them through his tailored shirt. I feel a hot flash coming on from the mere thought, so I keep my eyes trained upon his.

He drums his fingers on the patio table and I look at them. They are long and slender, but very manly at the same time. He's got sexy hands. I sigh. Why would they be anything else? They're attached to a sexy body.

Focus, imbecile! I reprimand myself. And I fixate on his eyes again.

Which of course doesn't help because he's got gorgeous eyes.

But I keep mine focused on them and ignore the way his full lips move as he speaks.

"Well, one of my good friends is a recruiter. And when he saw this position, he thought it would be a perfect fit for me. He knew that I'd been wanting to make a change. I really kind of wanted a complete and total new start."

I stare at him.

"Are you from here?"

"Yes," Alex answers as he takes a drink of wine. "But after my divorce, I moved across town and sort of changed my life in every way. I've started some hobbies, made some healthy changes... stuff like that. Sometimes, when you're married, you forget to grow as an individual because you're so focused on being part of a unit."

"How long ago were you divorced?" I ask curiously. For some reason, I had it in my head that it had been awhile.

"Eighteen months," he says. "And I'm all the better for it."

I sip at my wine, too. God, I love wine.

"What happened? Why did you divorce?"

"We grew apart," he shrugs. "I thought we were fine, and apparently, my wife was fine... but she was fine with her tennis instructor. So...we divorced. I'm not one of those freaks who likes to share my wife."

He grins wryly and I want to hug him suddenly. I certainly know what it feels like to get cheated on. But who in their right mind would cheat on Alex Harris?? Holy cow, what a silly wench his ex must be.

"My ex cheated too," I tell him. "And it was hard. I mean, it makes you re-examine everything about your life. But I'm better for it, too."

He's staring at me with an expression of total shock.

"Who in their right mind would cheat on you?" he asks candidly.

"That's exactly what I was just thinking about you!" I admit. "I guess our exes were just insane. So, here's to crazy." I clink my glass to his.

He smiles. "Well, crazy does have some benefits," he says. "If they hadn't lost their minds, we'd still be attached to them right?"

Yep, I think. *And I wouldn't be sitting here with you, practically drooling.*

Okay. I've got to put an end to these kinds of thoughts. He's my boss. I can't get involved with him. But I can't seem to convince my brain to stop thinking about him.

So I do the only thing I can think of to stop the madness...the only thing that might quell the insatiable need I have to act like an idiot around him.

I admit my infatuation to him.

Yes, I'm probably crazy. But I've known that for a while now.

"So, I'm improving myself too," I tell him, filling up our wine glasses yet again. "And one of the things that I'm doing is that I'm being completely honest about everything in my life. It takes too much energy to play games- and life is too short. So, I'm struggling with something here and I just want you to know about it. Because maybe that will help."

Alex stares at me in concern. "I'll help you in any way that I can, Alli."

"Okay, looking at me so sweetly is not helping," I announce. Since we're on my patio and into our third glass of wine, it's easy to lose sight of the fact that he's my boss.

"I'm not following you," Alex tells me uncertainly. "Have I offended you? I thought you said that you aren't easily offended."

"No, of course not," I tell him, sucking in a breath. "I'm not offended. I'm attracted to you. That's why I'm been acting like a bumbling idiot, I guess. You intimidate me and I'm attracted to you. And I don't agree with dating in the workplace because it makes things too awkward, so I'm sort of at a loss."

Now he's staring at me silently. And he looks a little shell-shocked, so I rush to apologize.

"Okay, I'm sorry. I crossed the line, didn't I?" I ask anxiously, my heart starting to pound. The last thing I need is to get fired for inappropriate behavior. Can this be considered inappropriate since it's in my own house? My thoughts race and my cheeks flush.

And then Alex smiles.

"That's a relief, actually. Because I'm attracted to you, too. And you intimidate me, as well. And I agree with not dating in the workplace."

This is so not what I expected.

I stare at him blankly, at a loss for what to say.

"And it's refreshing to talk to a woman who is so honest. I think that makes me even more intimidated, though."

Alex smiles again, and I swear to god—his teeth are so white! Is that even natural??

I'm still dumbfounded and Alex prompts me.

"Aren't you going to say anything?"

"I need more wine," I stammer, reaching for my glass. I take a sip. And look at him again. "You're intimidated by me? Why?"

He shrugs, all handsome and elegant and refined. "I don't know. I just am. I've gotten over it a little now, though. I think it was the whole vacuuming my crotch in front of you thing."

I flush again.

How can one woman manage to be one-hundred different kinds of idiotic?

"I don't know how that happened," I tell him again. "I really don't. Like I said, I've turned into a bumbling idiot around you. I feel like a freaking teenager."

He leans toward me conspiratorially. "I kind of do, too," he admits. "But we work together. And we're adults. We can handle it, right?"

I nod automatically. "Of course. I just thought it was fair to tell you why I seem to be acting so strangely. It feels sort of good to take the bull by the balls and just deal with a situation, rather than pussy-foot around."

Alex sighs. "It doesn't help when you use the words 'balls' and 'pussy' in the same sentence, Alli." He laughs now and I have to laugh too.

"This is the strangest conversation that I've ever had with a boss," I tell him. "But then, I've never had a crush on a boss before, so this is new territory. I feel sort of like I'm at tea with the Mad Hatter right now."

"Well, I might be the Mad Hatter, but at least I have underwear on," Alex deadpans.

"I have underwear on!" I announce. "I *usually* have underwear on. I just didn't that particular day for a very particular reason that I don't want to get into right now. And I think we should change the subject before I combust."

Alex grins.

"Agreed. Okay...how about kids? I saw a picture of your daughter. She's beautiful and looks like she could be your sister. Is she your only child?"

I nod. "Yes. Sophie. She's fifteen and my only. She's a great kid. She should probably be getting home from Cheerleading any time now, actually. How about you?"

"I just have one, as well. One son. He's twenty-three and apparently, he's still figuring his life out but he's a great kid too. He'll get it someday, I'm sure."

And then my doorbell rings. I can hear it through the screen of my patio doors.

"Dinner is served!" I announce with a smile. We take our glasses and return to the house. We eat our food curled up in the living room while we make some more small talk. And honestly, for once, I think I did something right. Telling Alex about my infatuation with him seemed to take some of the power away from it. I'm not nearly so intimated now.

Alex is interesting and engaging. And when the tow—truck arrives and he has to leave, I find that I am disappointed. And that is startling.

Which brings me to another fact that is startling.

I have a very definite crush on my boss.

Chapter Eighteen

(Or: Temptation, you are the devil. And I probably love you.)

Since Rick the Dick couldn't find it in his schedule to take Sophie for an extra night, I arrange to have Sara stay the night at our house with her. I'm fairly comfortable with that, or at least, I am after I stipulate that Sara can in no way do anything wild with Sophie.

My best friend solemnly promised.

So, I leave for the airport feeling somewhat at ease with the situation. I've also got an appointment scheduled with Shade for tomorrow night. I figure a hot, sexy date with a hot and sexy younger man will help take my mind off the fact that I have a crush on Alex. Shade could take a dying woman's mind off of the fate of her own soul. He's distracting that way.

I park my car and walk into the terminal...the one where they fly out the private planes. Zellers has its own fleet of private jets. Since I'm not a vice president of the company, I can only use them when I am traveling with a vice president. But it's still a nice perk.

Alex is already here, waiting for me. He looks stunningly handsome in his casual khakis and white button-up. Sara was most certainly right. White button-ups can be hot as hell after all, particularly when stretched across his toned chest.

And as if looking so good wasn't gift enough to me this early in the morning, he hands me a cup of gourmet coffee. Is he trying to make me fall in love with him? Geez.

"Thank you," I tell him, sipping at the nectar of the Gods. "I didn't have time to stop on the way."

"I didn't figure you would," he tells me. "Are you ready?"

I nod. "I am. I stayed up last night and reviewed the email you sent. Everything looks in order."

"It is," he agrees. "This should go smoothly. I think this project is going to work and they're going to be naming conference rooms after us at work." He grins and I grin back, both at his cockiness and at the thought of my name on a plaque outside of a plush conference room at Zellers.

I follow him up the stairs and into the plane, where we are surrounded by the kind of luxury that usually only senior executives are afforded. Plush leather couches, soft blankets, private flight attendants. I decide that I need a promotion so that I can fly like this even when I'm not accompanied by Alex. Vice president is only one step up from my current executive director title, after all.

The flight is only thirty minutes long, so we really don't even have time to settle in and get comfortable before we're touching down in San Diego. There's a car waiting for us, a sleek black Town Car, which takes us to our hotel.

"I figured we could meet up in my room to go over a few things and then we could go to dinner," Alex suggests as the car glides to a stop and the driver opens the door.

"Sure," I tell him, even though being cooped up with Alex in his room sends my heart into palpations. "Just let me put my bag in my room first."

We check in and I head to my room. The hotel is amazing and my room has a gorgeous view of the ocean. I shoot a quick email from my phone to Taylor to thank her. She really does take care of me and I know she's trying to make up for sending Alex to my house yesterday.

At the thought, I touch my face. The swelling has gone down a remarkable amount. Seriously, you can barely tell now. My eyes look like they are a little puffy from lack of sleep, not like someone took a ball-bat to my cheekbones. It's progress and I'll take it.

I drop my suitcase and look into the bathroom mirror.

I look pretty good, actually, all things considered. I pull a brush through my hair and glide some lip balm on and then I make my way to Alex's room, which is just down the hall.

He opens the door and I have to suck in my breath. He's loosened the collar of his shirt, which makes him look even sexier. Heaven help me.

"Hey," he greets me. "How about this view?"

"I know," I answer as I step inside. "If only Vegas had an ocean, right?"

"Well, we've got a desert. That's almost as good, right?" he flashes me a grin. A white, white grin. I steel my resolve. "Can I get you something to drink?"

"A water would be great," I tell him as I take a seat at the table. He's already got papers spread out everywhere, even though we've only been here for fifteen minutes. He hands me the bottle and then sits next to me.

He smells like the outdoors...like sunshine and man. And I find myself wanting to leap into his lap and inhale him. Which would be weird. So I resist the urge and instead, I focus on the paperwork in front of us. It keeps us occupied for two hours, actually.

And I find that once we start talking business, I am able to somehow tune out his sexiness and his amazing smell and focus on the matters at hand. We come up with a pretty spectacular co-partnership model to present in the morning, if I do say so myself.

"We're a good team," Alex points out as he starts gathering the papers together. I nod.

"Yes, we are."

"Are you in the mood for steak?" he asks. "Because I am."

I smile. "Are men always in the mood for steak?"

He nods. "Yes."

"Well, in that case, far be it from me to keep you from exhibiting your man hood. If you want to beat on your chest for a second, I'll wait patiently."

Alex laughs and my vagina flutters.

He slips on his shoes and then holds open the door, a perfect gentleman. I find myself mesmerized by his movements, by everything about him, actually. I gulp.

This whole working together thing is harder than I even anticipated. Why does he have to be so gorgeous? BB flutters again, her vaginal antennae on high alert. I shush her. Now is definitely not the time.

Before I know it, we are seated in an elegant dining room, in the dark corner of a restaurant that has soft music piped in the background. I have a glass of red wine and Alex has a gin and tonic. And I am losing myself in his blue eyes.

It doesn't help that there is a decorative mirror on the wall next to us and when I glance at it, I can see that we look perfect together. Perfect ages, perfect differences in height and even our coloring complements each other. I turn my attention back to him. This isn't helping.

"So," I begin, "What do you think of Zellers so far?"

He temples his fingers, something that I notice he does when he is restless.

"Zellers is a great company," he tells me. "It's full of talented and energetic people. Honestly, I'm impressed by everyone that I've met so far. And your department is the most impressive of all. You certainly know what you're doing."

The compliment turns my cheeks pink.

It's true. I am successful and good at my job. And to have someone like him, someone who is also successful and good at his job, notice... well, it just feels good.

"Thank you," I murmur. "I try."

"You do more than try," he answers, taking another drink. "Head-hunters from miles away have noticed you. Can you give me your word that you won't consider leaving until you've talked to me about it?"

I'm surprised now.

"None have approached me," I tell him honestly. "And I love Zellers. It will take an unbelievably good package to entice me to leave."

He smiles at me. "Great. That's exactly what I wanted to hear."

We continue chatting all through our meal and then we share a piece of chocolate cake for dessert. After he wipes his mouth and tosses his napkin onto his plate, Alex looks at me.

"I haven't eaten that much in a long time. Would you like to take a walk on the beach? I'd like to get some air."

"Of course," I tell him, pushing back my chair. And within a minute, I find myself under the full moon, walking with this gorgeous man beside the crashing ocean.

Not the smartest thing to do, Alli, I reprimand myself. I should be avoiding these types of situations, not creating more of them.

But it feels so good to have my arm looped through his, to talk about intelligent topics that we both understand because we're both in the same industry. It feels amazing to be with someone who understands me for exactly who I am… a woman who is just trying to make a new life and get ahead at work.

He understands because he is exactly the same… my perfect male counter-part.

I gulp. And then gulp harder.

I could be walking with my perfect match.

As he guides me around a big piece of driftwood, I have to acknowledge that my idea of telling him about my infatuation wasn't that effective after all. In fact, things have only gotten worse. Knowing that he feels the same way about me makes the temptation that much harder to resist.

"Is this as hard for you as it is for me?" Alex asks softly, as though he can read my freaking mind. I nod silently. He stops walking and stares at me. The light from the moon shines onto him and I swear to all that is holy, he looks like a freaking GQ model.

"Yes," I tell him. "It definitely is. And were you ever, at any time, a GQ model perchance?"

He stares down at me and I can't help but notice his rock hard chest, his flat abs, his chiseled features. How could Mother Nature have done this to me? She put my perfect match in my life, but made him my boss? Is she a masochist?

Alex smiles and then tucks a tuft of my hair behind my ear.

"No, I wasn't," he answers with a grin. "But I'll take it as a compliment that you think I could have been."

"It might not have been a compliment," I announce. "Models are, by nature, over-confident and cocky."

Alex studies me, then grins.

"I don't know about that," he says. "I've heard that they are sometimes secretly insecure and just need approval. And that sometimes, they get intimidated by people who are better-put-together than they are."

I'm not sure, but I think that last part was in reference to me. I swallow hard.

"It was a compliment," I admit. "You're gorgeous. And sexy as hell. And I'm struggling a little bit."

"I am too. But we can do this," he says quietly. "We can work together and be completely professional. I have faith in us."

Us.

I want to leap into his arms and kiss him with tongue. No lie.

His mouth is just so tantalizing. And there is something about a powerful and important man that turns me on. BB is practically salivating, but I ignore her silent pleadings.

"Yes," I agree. "We can. I'm sure this infatuation will pass."

He looks as unsure as I feel. But we continue on our walk and to my intense pride, I don't invite myself back to his room when we get back to the hotel. I return to my own like a responsible adult.

We get up the next morning and totally rock our meeting.

It goes as smoothly as any business meeting has ever gone. Plus, I managed to avoid doing anything embarrassing for once. That's a miracle in itself.

As we fly home, we chit-chat about non-important things and I am able to utterly ignore the way I want to drape myself across his lap and stick my tongue in his mouth. My tongue is still a hussy, apparently.

When I reach my house, I find that nothing is amiss. Sara has had an uneventful evening with Sophie and in fact, even left a basket of fresh fruit on my counter.

And, last but certainly not least, I have a date with Shade tonight. If he can't distract me from my thoughts about Alex, nothing will.

****

As I'm getting ready, I text Shade.

I need a good distraction. Think of something kinky to do tonight.

My fingers are almost shaking as I put my phone down, but I ignore it. I've got to try new things. That's the point of all of this, right? And it's going to take something new to drive Alex from my mind.

How kinky? Shade texts back.

Kinky, I answer. I'm so insane. I know that.

Don't worry, then. I've got a plan, Shade replies.

And now my fingers shake. A plan? Good lord. But he's a good kid and I trust him. And so I find myself looking forward to tonight as I finish getting dressed. Little black dress, black heels and my hair pulled into a sleek low-pony.

When I walk into the room at Utopia later, though, and Shade takes off the blindfold and I see an extra man standing there, I can't help but get a little nervous.

I turn to Shade.

"What exactly is your plan?"

My fingers are shaking with abandon now and my legs are twitching. I almost want to spin on my high-heels and take off at a dead sprint for my car.

Shade touches my elbow in a comforting way.

"Calm down, Alli Cat," he murmurs. "I know you trust me. I wouldn't do anything that I know you wouldn't like."

"Well, what if you don't know that I wouldn't like it?" I challenge.

I eye the other man. He's tall. Dark. Handsome. My exact type. But still.

My heart pounds.

"I'm not doing a threesome," I tell Shade.

"And I'm not either," he answers. "You just came back from a business trip, right? And so I assume that you're a little tense. Every woman likes a good massage. And Tyler here just happens to be a certified masseuse. I'm going to blindfold you. Tyler is going to massage you. And I'm going to do...other things to you. You're going to feel a bunch of hands on you and even though I'll be the only having sex with you, it won't seem like it. It's a safe way to get all the excitement of a threesome, without the actual threesome."

I eye him.

I have to admit, I like the idea. It's naughty. And it might be just what I need as a distraction.

"You're the only one who will be having sex with me?" I ask.

Shade nods. "Of course. I'm not sharing you, Alli Cat."

His words comfort me. And at this moment, I realize that I've allowed him to become my crutch. He's my safe comfort. I pay him to do what I want. I'm controlling the situation which means that I might be limiting my life. But I shake the troublesome thoughts away. I'll worry about that later. Right now, I have a fake threesome to attend to.

"Take off your clothes and put this blind-fold on," Shade says. "Then lie on the bed."

Tyler smiles at me from across the room and he's gorgeous. In all honesty, I can't wait for him to touch me. His hands are long and sexy...just my type of hands.

My heart pounds.

I'm definitely going to burn in hell.

But that doesn't stop me from stripping off my clothes and climbing on the bed buck-ass naked before pulling on the blindfold.

Almost immediately, Tyler is sliding hot oil on my skin and I don't even have to worry about it staining the sheets because it isn't my bed. And it feels amazing. He's murmuring to me about how fit I am, how beautiful I am. He rubs my shoulders, my arms, my calves. He pays close attention to the tension in my neck and I lean into his hands.

"Tyler, I think I love you," I say. He laughs softly and moves down to my thighs.

And then I feel another set of hands.

They caress my belly before lips follow suit. Kisses are trailed across my abdomen, up to my neck and back down to my thighs. Tyler continues to rub me and pretty soon, all of the hands seem to run together, just like Shade said that that they would.

It's naughty.

It's erotic.

It's *amazing.*

I moan a little and Shade bends to my ear.

"Do you like it, Alli Cat?" he whispers. As he does, he slips a finger inside of me. At least, I'm pretty sure it is him. I know it is, but it is fun to tell myself that it might be Tyler.

I nod. "Yes," I whisper.

It's so unbelievably sexy and hot to know that Shade is fingering me in front of another man. I can't even believe how turned on it makes me. And how willing I am to let him do it. It looks like there certainly is a cougar buried in me. It just took her a few years to come out.

Shade's tongue is lapping at my breasts, then he kisses my neck before I feel the weight of his strong body on top of mine. I grip his hips, which flex beneath my fingers.

There is a rustle of foil, which surprises me because I can still feel Tyler rubbing me...my calves, my thighs, my hips.

And then Shade is against me and then in me. I gasp, and buck against him. Tyler is still rubbing me, fondling me, caressing me. Hands are everywhere.

Shade slides in...then out. In...then out. It's excruciatingly slow, but it allows me to focus on the way Tyler is caressing me, too. It's unbelievably erotic.

"I'm going to hell," I mutter into Shade's ear.

He laughs.

"Well, if that's true, then we'd better make it worth it."

He pulls out and flips me over, onto my hands and knees.

As he does, there is a mouth on my breast....a mouth that can't possibly be Shade since he is behind me. I gasp as a tongue circles my nipple, then slides it into a mouth. A faceless mouth, but a mouth that I am sure is Tyler's.

"Anytime you want to stop, say pineapple," Shade reminds me.

I nod but remain silent.

Because I like it.

Because I am a shameless, shameless hussy. The naughtiness of this situation is thrilling.

One set of hands grips my hips, pulling me into his own as he slides in and out of me. *Shade.* The other set of hands caresses me everywhere, setting all of my nerve endings on fire. *Tyler.*

Oh, lord I am a dirty, dirty woman.

"Say my name," Shade instructs me.

"Shade," I cry out as he plunges deep inside.

"Say it louder," he tells me. I can see only the velvet blackness of the blindfold as I do what he says.

"Shade!" I shout. My breath is ragged, my voice is harsh.

And it only takes me two more minutes to come because there is a set of hands down below, rubbing circles on BB, who incidentally, is crowing silently in delight. She's a bigger hussy than I am, apparently.

I fall limply to the bed and then pull my blindfold off.

Tyler is lying behind me, Shade is lying in front of me. I am lying in the middle of two beautiful and young men. I feel like a painting from ancient Greece titled *Woman in the middle of an orgy.* The room might as well go up in flames now so that I can get used to the fires of hell. I sigh and curve into Shade's body.

"Well, I asked for kinky," I say wryly.

"And you know that we have a 100% customer satisfaction policy here at Utopia," Shade grins, a lazy smile that makes BB perk to attention again already. Like I said, BB is a shameless hussy. "I wouldn't want you to ask for your money back."

I laugh, but his words only serve to remind me once again that I am paying him. I am controlling the situation. I am closing myself to real opportunities that might exist for me out in the real world.

Opportunities like Alex.

But I shut that annoying inner voice up by sitting up and smiling confidently at the two men next to me.

"Who is up for a shower?" I ask brightly.

Shade cocks an eyebrow. "You're asking both of us?"

I nod what I hope is a confident and sex-vixen-ish nod.

"I'm just asking for a shower," I say innocently.

Shade grins in reply, as does Tyler.

"I've rubbed off on you, Alli Cat. You're quite the pupil."

I slide from the bed and grab his hands, pulling him with me to the bathroom. Tyler trails behind on his own accord, closing the bathroom door as he enters.

"Well, a pupil is only as good as her teacher," I purr, running my hands up and down Shade's flat, strong chest.

But as Tyler turns on the water in the shower and I step in with Shade, the only thing I can see is Alex's face for a second. It's startling and I gasp.

"Are you alright?" Tyler asks me in concern. I nod.

"Yes, I'm fine. The water just wasn't warm yet."

But that's a lie. The water was perfectly warm. And so are my cheeks as I realize that I'm thinking of Alex while I'm showering with two young, gorgeous men. If I had wanted to have a real threesome, which I most certainly do not, those desires would have been dashed at these unexpected thoughts of Alex.

So, instead, I block out images of him and just enjoy being washed by two attentive men. Tyler washes my front, Shade washes my back. And they are both pressed against me, wet and slippery and hard.

Holy Freaking Hotness.

But we only take a shower. I meant what I said. I don't quite feel comfortable enough with the situation to use Tyler's "services". Even still, it's a very sexy situation. These guys are gorgeous and sexy and very good at their jobs. This is a memory that will forever live in infamy in my mind.

But as Shade pats me dry with a big, fluffy towel, I find myself imagining that his hands are Alex's hands. And I sigh a very long sigh.

I'm seriously, definitely, most certainly in trouble.

Chapter Nineteen

(Or: Fate is a Twisted, Sick Wench)

"Omigod. You're so going to hell," Sara exclaims into my phone as pull on a robe the next morning and stumble to the kitchen to make coffee. "*I* wouldn't even do that. Well, maybe I would. But I haven't *yet*."

I roll my eyes. "You so would. Your little guy, Chaz, just hasn't thought of trying it yet with you. You should mention it to him. I know you'd like it."

"Honey, I would rock the hell out of that shit," Sara says and I know that she has already mentally added it to her list of things to do."

I pour the coffee into the maker as I listen to her ramble.

"So, you didn't actually have sex with the second one?" she asks, a little incredulous. I giggle.

"No. I sort of actually wanted to... but that would be crossing a line for me, I think. I can only go so far until I feel like I'm getting out of control. But it was still fun. I felt really naughty."

"You *were* really naughty," she answers. "Ooh- have you ever thought of getting spanked?? A naughty girl should be spanked. And you're welcome. If it weren't for me, you'd still be twiddling your thumbs all by yourself on the weekends."

"Thank you, Sara," I answer obligingly. "You're right. You have expanded my horizons but not far enough to get spanked. I'm pretty sure I wouldn't enjoy that."

I hit the brew button and then collapse into a kitchen chair.

It's 10:00 am and I'm only just now getting up. But to be fair, I didn't get home until after 2:00 am. Sophie stayed the night with Hayley again and she's not home yet, so there's no reason I needed to be up earlier.

Sara chatters into my ear for a while and I don't know why, but I decide to tell her about Alex and how I couldn't even keep him out of my thoughts last night when I was with Shade and Tyler. She is silent in astonishment for a moment after I am through.

"Omigod," she says again for the fortieth time today. "You're falling for your boss. Like, really falling for him."

"Maybe," I tell her. "He just seems so right for me. And he's so hilarious. You know how I love a good sense of humor. Plus, we're in the same exact position in life. It's uncanny. But I just don't think I can bring myself to date anyone right now. That's how you talked me into the whole Shade thing, remember? Because I wasn't ready to date."

"Yes, but Shade was meant as a way to ease you into the dating world. I figured if you had sex with someone, it would take the stress out of getting into a real relationship eventually. It's been nine months since the divorce, Alli. And you were in therapy for a year before that, trying to figure everything out. You've worked on yourself, you've given yourself time. If there is someone there who seems to be everything you want, you shouldn't hesitate to reach out and grab him by the balls."

"You make him sound like he is ripe apricot at the grocery," I tell her grumpily. "Except for the balls part. You don't get it. He's my boss. I'm afraid to date anyone right now. I put fifteen years into my relationship with Rick only to have him cheat on me and trash everything we worked for."

Sara snorts. "Rick didn't work for anything. *You* did all the work. You worked on the relationship, you worked to earn enough money for him to start his own business…. *You* worked. He didn't. It's time for you to date a real man."

I'm silent as I think about that.

But my moment of reflection is interrupted by the doorbell.

"Hey, I've got to go," I tell Sara. "I'll call you later."

I pad to the door and peer through, only to find Rick the Dick himself standing on my porch. Holy crap. Speak of the devil.

I open the door.

"Yes? Sophie isn't here. Were you supposed to pick her up?"

I'm confused. No one told me anything of the sort. But he is already shaking his head.

"No. I'm actually here to see you. Can I come in?"

Rick is uncharacteristically quiet and subdued. And now I'm even more confused.

"Sure. Come in, I guess."

I open the door wider and he walks past, walking straight for the kitchen. He takes a seat at the table.

"Can you sit?" He motions to an empty seat across from him. I try not to feel resentful that he is controlling the situation in my own house. Instead, I draw my robe more tightly closed and sit down.

"What's going on?" I ask him, eyeing him suspiciously. "What do you want?"

He rolls his eyes.

"I don't want anything, Allison," he sighs. "Isn't it possible that I just want to have a conversation with you? We used to talk all the time."

I stare at him.

"Yes, we did," I acknowledge. "Before I found out that you had cheated on me for years. That sort of burns the bridges of communication."

He almost scowls before he quickly hides it. And this makes me even more suspicious. He's trying very hard to be nice, which means he wants to ask me for something.

"What do you want?" I ask again. "I haven't had any coffee yet, so I'm afraid I'm a little impatient."

As if on cue, my coffee maker beeps to signal that it is done. Rick stands up and walks to it, pulling down a cup from the cupboard. He pours in coffee, cream and sugar and hands it back to me.

"See?" he says with a smile. "I know how you like things, Alli."

And now I'm on edge. His tone is strange, almost flirty. My eyes narrow.

"Allison, I've made a mistake. I think it's because I was going through a mid-life crisis. But I miss being home with you and Sophie. I think we should get back together and give it another try."

He just throws it out there like he's talking about a football game, like it's even in the realm of possibility. Which it isn't.

I'm left with my mouth open.

"Wha—what?" I ask stupidly.

Rick smiles. "I'd like to get back together."

"What about Vanessa?" I ask, because in my haze, it's the only thing I can think of to say.

Rick shrugs. "She's a nice girl, but she's too immature. I miss you, Allison. I miss the way you took care of me."

And that's it right there. He misses being taken care of. His little Vanessa needs someone to take care of *her* so there's no way she can take care of him. This isn't about me at all, it's about *him*. Of course. Just like always. My blood instantly boils, so I count to ten before I speak.

"I don't think so, Rick."

And now he's the one who is astonished. "What?"

"You cheated on me," I bite out through clenched teeth. "You humiliated me in front of everyone we know by cheating on me with girls who are barely older than teenagers. And now you are engaged to one. I wish you the best, but that certainly won't be with me."

"Now, Alli," he says soothingly, putting a hand on my arm. I pull it away and glare at him. "Think of Sophie," he adds. "She can have her family back."

I glare at him harder. "I can't believe you're even saying these words. You are the reason this family isn't together right now. You. You cheated. You tore us apart. And now I've moved on. Get out."

He looks at me. "Alli, come on—" But I interrupt him. "Get. Out."

He scowls as he shoves his chair back, scraping the tiled floor. "If I walk out right now, Alli, I'm not coming back. I won't offer again."

I am dumbfounded as I stand up.

"You coming back is not an offer, you ass. It's a threat. Please leave. And don't come back here unless it is to pick up Sophie. I don't want anything to do with you."

He stalks out and I lock the door after him before sliding to the ground, shaking like a leaf. How in the hell would he ever think that I would take him back...ever? What a pompous, self-absorbed ass.

I text Sara from the floor in a foul-mouthed text that leaves me feeling better. I tuck my phone back into my robe pocket as I continue back into the kitchen and drink my coffee. What a way to kick off my weekend. But between my text conversation with Sara and Sophie coming home, I am distracted.

Sophie and I go shopping, get take-out and basically, just have a girl's weekend again. And my thoughts are deflected from thinking about Alex, which is exactly what I wanted to happen.

That is, until that night when I am getting ready for bed and I get a text from him.

Even though I shouldn't be, I'm thinking about you.

My insides melt and I fall into bed, yanking the covers up and over my head. What the hell am I going to do?

Monday comes all too soon and I don't have any answers by then, either. I do take extra care getting ready for work. I dress in a pale gray pencil skirt, a pale pink silk blouse and dark gray heels. The skirt makes my ass look fabulous and the silk shirt clings to my girls. I know that I look good as I stride into my office.

Taylor looks up and smiles.

"Morning, boss!" She hands me a stack of messages. "There's fresh coffee on your desk."

Oh, how I love that girl.

But when I reach my desk, I see the local coffee house cup and I know that it wasn't Taylor. It was Alex. He's been bringing me this coffee because he knows I like it. My insides melt again as I drop into my chair.

It feels good to be taken care of, even in this small way.

I open up my email and sift through them, answering a few and deleting a few others. And then Taylor knocks softly on my office door.

"Hey, boss. Your new intern is here."

Her face looks strange and I raise my eyebrow.

"What?" I ask her. She takes a step into my office and lowers her voice.

"He's freaking hot," she whispers. "He's going to be quite the distraction in the workplace. You can expect productivity to decrease ten-fold with him here."

I roll my eyes. Taylor is in her twenties, so a twenty-three year old intern probably will be a distraction for her.

"Are you going to be able to control yourself?" I ask jokingly. "You've got to figure out things for him to do."

"Oh, I can think of some things for him to do," she says lasciviously, and then laughs. I roll my eyes again .

"Just show him in before you pounce on him, please. The last thing we need is a sexual harassment suit."

She grins and is gone. And then she's back within a minute. It takes me a second to realize that the shadow following her is Colby.

As in... Shade.

What.

The.

Hell.

I am staring at him with my mouth open as Sara introduces him to me. But I barely hear her voice. The sound is roaring in my ears. I'm just flabbergasted. And Colby's grin is mischievous, his eyes sparkling. It's almost as if he knew, like he was expecting to see me.

I stand up stiffly, holding my hand out.

"Hi Colby. It's nice to see you again," I say for Taylor's benefit. I shake the hand that has been everywhere on my body, the fingers that have been inside of my mouth...and other places. My eyes never leave his and the ornery expression never disappears from his face.

He knew.

I am sure of it.

"You already know each other?" Taylor is surprised as she stares at me.

My eyes haven't left Colby's. "Yes. Colby is Sophie's new swim coach."

"Ah," Taylor answers, practically fawning over Colby. "That makes sense. You look like a swimmer," she tells him. He grins at her.

"Thank you, Taylor," I tell her. "I'll just take a few minutes to talk with Colby about the position. Can you close my door?"

She looks intrigued, but she does as I ask and I am alone with Colby.

I fight to stay calm as the ramifications of this scenario hit home with me.

Colby is Shade.

Shade is a gigolo whom I slept with.

Shade's father is Alex who I have a crush on.

Oh, sweet Lord.

My life is an endless series of complications.

"You knew," I say softly. "You knew when you came in here today that I would be here, didn't you?"

Colby grins, his blue eyes sparkling.

"Yes. My dad called last week and gave me your name so that I would know who to ask for."

In a valiant effort to hold my shit together, I take three deep breaths before answering him.

"And you didn't say anything to me on Friday night because?" I raise an eyebrow now and swallow hard as I remember what we did together on Friday.

"Because I thought it would be fun to surprise you," he admits, taking a step toward me. I take a step back, then in fact, I retreat behind my desk. There is laughter in his eyes when I meet his gaze.

"Alli, why are you running from me?" His blue eyes are sparkling. "This doesn't change anything. In fact, I only took this position after my dad told me who to ask for. I have to admit, I thought it would be fun to work here with you. But that doesn't change our weekend activities. You've seen me coach Sophie. I'm very good at compartmentalizing things. I can handle everything. Trust me."

He's so cute. So, so cute.

And so, so young.

Did I mention so, so young?

I make a decision, on the spot, without even consulting BB and I know she will kill me later.

I also know that I might live to regret it, but I know I have to do it.

And seriously, as I gaze at him, at how young and gorgeous he is, my resolve wavers. But then I remember that I can't keep paying him to fill a void in my life. Because as long as I do that, I won't move forward and find something real.

So, I sigh while BB silently wails. I know that if she could, she'd be punching me in the pelvic floor right now.

"Colby, you are adorable. And we've had a lot of fun. But this does complicate things. But even still, I do believe that this is a great opportunity for you while you're figuring out what you want to do in life. So, I'm going to end our...other relationship. It's fulfilled its purpose anyway. I needed you to get me ready to date again. And you have. So, thank you. It's been really fun."

Colby stares at me, all amusement gone from his eyes now. In fact, I see dismay there as he realizes what I'm saying. And honestly, I can't quite believe I'm saying it.

Am I seriously going to break up the perfect arrangement for something that may or may not ever happen?

But I picture Alex's handsome face and I steel my resolve.

Yes. I am.

"It's been really fun? Alli, come on. I promise. I can handle this. No one will ever know that we know each other from elsewhere."

"Oh, I know," I tell him. "But see, that's the problem. *I* will know. And I know that you won't say anything. But I'm not as good at compartmentalizing as you are. I can't continue to see you and work with you here. I'm not that talented."

Colby throws his head back and laughs now. "Alli, you're far more talented than you think."

I shake my head. "See? This is what I'm talking about. If you throw sexual innuendoes at me, I can't concentrate on work. And I'm here to work during the day. Plus, having you and your dad both here is just twenty different kinds of wrong if I'm still seeing you. So I'm not going to."

Colby is quiet as he assesses me.

"My dad. You know, when you told me that you needed distracting, I wondered if it was because you may have met someone. Were you talking about my dad?"

I hesitate for a moment too long before answering, because Colby almost gasps.

"You were."

I nod.

"You have a thing for my dad," Colby says slowly as if he's trying to make himself understand it.

"I might," I say. "I'm trying to figure that out."

Colby shakes his head. "Well, I've taught you well. At least I know my dad will be taken care of." He laughs because he means it as a joke. But I shudder.

"See? This is all just too weird," I say, feeling a little sick to my stomach. "I can't date your dad now. There's no way in the world. And does your dad know what you do?"

I sink into my chair, my head in my hands. Why does my life have to be so messed up?

Colby comes around and massages my shoulders lightly.

"No, my dad doesn't know what I do. And *yes*, Alli, you can date my dad. In fact, I talked to him yesterday on the phone and he sounded happier than he has sounded in a long time. I asked him if a woman was to blame for that and he told me that he had met someone, but that he couldn't date her because it was complicated."

I nod miserably. "It's even more complicated than he knows. And this isn't helping," I answer.

Colby stops massaging my shoulders and bends, looking me in the eye.

"Alli, I know my father and I know you. You are perfect for each other. I know it seems strange, but we'll stop seeing each other and after a while, we'll practically forget that we were ever a thing. It won't be a big deal at all."

"But I don't know if I can date your dad knowing that I slept with his son," I practically whisper. Saying it out loud makes it sound so seedy and horrible and dramatic, like I should be on a bad soap opera.

Colby rolls his eyes.

"Alli, my dad will never know. And you didn't sleep with his son. You slept with Shade. My dad's son is Colby. We're two different people. And my dad will never, ever know."

"You might be two different people, but you share the same penis," I remind him wryly. Colby laughs.

"Either way. My sex life isn't my dad's concern. People don't need to disclose who they've had sex with in the past. It will be fine, Alli. And I can't believe that I have to stand here and talk to you like this. You and my dad need to figure it out. It's stupid to let a job get in the way of happiness."

I stare at him. "How did you get so smart for a twenty-three year old?"

He just smiles, a young and handsome grin.

"I guess it's a family trait. Now, Alli Cat, changing the subject...what are you going to have me do here at Zellers?"

I square my shoulders, back to business.

"Well, first, I'll tell you what you won't be doing. You won't be calling me Alli Cat. Someone might hear you."

Colby grins. "I promise. When I walk out that door, I will pretend that the only way I know you is through your daughter. But in here," and he taps his temple. "You will always be Alli Cat."

I sigh.

"Taylor will be your supervisor," I tell him. "Not me. I mean, you'll ultimately report to me, but Taylor will oversee your duties. I think she's lined up some marketing research for you to do. She's interesting and very good at her job. And she's every bit as much of a firecracker as my friend Sara is, so may God have mercy on your soul."

He's laughing as he walks out to see Taylor.

And I'm dropping my head back into my hands.

What a freaking mess.

Chapter Twenty

(Or: Decisions will be the effing death of me)

Colby is quite a hit in the office.

Every time I walk out of my own office for anything, I see the women (young and old) staring at him discreetly. He seems to be oblivious to it, but surely he has to know. He has to feel all of those pairs of eyes glued to his every movement. But then again, he's probably used to it.

Oddly enough, I'm not jealous. It's that realization that lets me know that I'm doing the right thing.

And every time I see him and Alex standing side by side, I *know* that I'm doing the right thing.

Colby is young and handsome and sexy.

Alex is older, refined and sexy. Every bit as handsome and twice the experience. He's what I need.

He's what I need.

The words resonate in my head.

And today, when Alex glances up and catches my eye, his cobalt gaze is warm and sparkling, like he knows a secret. And I see now why I kept thinking he looked familiar. He and his son share the same exact eyes. I don't know how I didn't place that trait before.

He slaps Colby on the back and makes his way over to me.

From behind him, Colby gives me a stare.

A *make-the-right-choice-you-idiot* stare.

I ignore it. I know that he's waiting for his father and I to make the leap—to throw caution to the wind and just openly begin dating. But that's a hard decision to make, for many different reasons.

As Alex walks towards me, Colby is acting like this is a moment of truth, a pivotal moment where I have to act. But that's not true. I can continue to take things slow. Alex will still be here. And I will be here.

But we still work together right now, which is a problem.

However, when Alex reaches me and I stare into his gorgeous eyes, I have to admit that I feel the pressure to make a decision....to somehow figure out how to make this work. Because there is such chemistry here, such a palpable attraction, that I'm not sure how much longer I want to resist it. Opportunities don't always knock more than once. I don't want to miss the chance to build a relationship with someone that is seemingly so perfect for me.

"I still can't get over that Colby is your daughter's swim coach," Alex says as he stops next to me. "What a small world."

I practically choke. He has no idea how small.

"Can I talk to you for a second?" he asks me quietly.

Taylor and Colby both pretend not to watch, but I can see them both gazing at us from the corner of their eyes as Alex and I step into my office.

"Of course," I say instead, closing my door firmly behind us. "Please, have a seat."

"In a minute," he says, striding toward me. He takes my face in his hands and crushes his lips to mine.

It is a consuming kiss that threatens to set my hair on fire.

I am gasping by the time it is over.

"I just needed to see," he murmurs as he steps away.

"See what?" I ask breathlessly. I am limp. I don't even know what to do.

"See if that would be as good as I imagined."

"And?" I breathe.

"Oh, it was better," he assures me. "Alli, we need to sort this thing out. I've been lying awake at night thinking about you. It can't be that difficult. You're attracted to me, I'm attracted to you. We're both adults. It's not rocket science."

"But we work together," I state simply. "It will be awkward."

"It will only be awkward if we make it that way," he answers firmly. "But how about this--go on a date with me. Let's see how we get along outside of the realm of work or business. And then, if we still feel the same way, we'll discuss all of these issues. There is no sense in worrying about it right now. We haven't even been on a date."

I stare at him.

"I think we'll still feel the same," I tell him softly, watching his lips. All I can do when I'm around him, apparently, is think of him sexually. It's crazy. I'm an adult, not a teenager.

But you're a dirty, dirty woman, BB reminds me. I ignore her. BB is a wanton tramp. What does she know?

"I think so too," Alex answers, taking another step toward me. I only have a brief second to inhale before his lips are covering mine again. My hands are on his back, which is muscular and broad, and I am melting into him. He tastes like mint and smells like man. His lips are soft and his arms are strong. And his penis is hard. I know it right now…I'm in serious trouble.

"This date you speak of," I say as he finally pulls away and I adjust my clothing. "When and where?"

Alex grins, an alarmingly breathtaking smile. He seems oblivious to the fact that his penis is so hard that it almost impaled my leg a second ago.

"Tonight. There's a little Italian restaurant on twenty-first street. Manini's. Do you know it?"

I stare at him in shock. It's the very same place I had suggested when Brainy Brian couldn't make a decision. It's too ironic.

"Yes. I love that place," I answer.

He smiles again, pleased. "Good. Why don't I pick you up at 7:00?"

I swallow. "Okay."

He closes in on me once again, crushing me to him. Once again, his rock-hard penis is against my hip. BB whimpers.

"Or we could make it a lunch date," he suggests in my ear. He smells so good and feels so amazing pressed against me that I can hardly think straight.

"Okay," I agree, without even thinking about what it would look like. I take a breath and pull away. "Wait. This is what I'm talking about. This is why it is complicated since we work together. People will see us leave. They'll know what we're doing."

He stares at me. "Do you care what people think?"

"Not usually," I admit. "But when they are my staff, I do care if they think I'm being unprofessional. Because then I won't have a leg to stand on if I have to reprimand them for the same thing at any given point."

"You're their boss," he reminds me. "You'll never have to reprimand them for leaving in the middle of the morning to have a date with their boss. Because *you're* their boss. And I'm pretty sure that you're going to be dating me."

I suck in breath. I love that he is so decisive.

"But we haven't even gone on a real date yet," I tell him. "You can't possibly know that."

He smiles. "I've got great intuition. Get your purse."

I'm frozen now as I look at him. "But it's only 10:00 am."

Alex nods. "I've changed my mind. We're going to brunch."

I have to chuckle, but I do as he says. I grab my purse. We walk nonchalantly out of my office and I stop to tell Taylor that Alex and I have a meeting outside of the building. Since she keeps my calendar, she knows that there is no such meeting.

But to her credit (and for once in her lifetime) she doesn't say anything. She just nods. Colby looks up from his cubicle knowingly, but he doesn't say anything, either, although I see a little smirk on his face as I pass by.

Alex and I make our way through the parking garage and honest-to-god we barely get into the car before we are practically attacking each other in the front seat.

Alex's hands are everywhere, his mouth is on my neck, on my lips. My hand finds its way to his crotch which is rock hard and straining against his pants. He groans when I touch him.

"You're making me crazy," he whispers. And I suddenly feel oh-so-powerful. This important man is groaning beneath my fingertips? It's a heady feeling. I kiss him hard.

His hand finds my breast, his fingers long and strong through the thin silk.

"We need to leave here," I tell him. We are surrounded by the dark, cement walls of the parking garage, but anyone could walk past and see into his car. And then we could get led away in handcuffs for indecent exposure or something. That would not be good.

"Yes," Alex agrees stiltedly. He shifts into Drive and my hand never leaves his crotch. In fact, as he drives out of the building, I am leaning over and unzipping his pants, the skin of my hand sliding across the skin of his penis. He sucks in his breath.

"Are you testing my concentration?" he asks feverishly. I glance at him, at the way his mouth has pulled tight and I laugh.

"Are you having trouble concentrating?" I ask innocently. He glances at me for a split second before he swerves over to the side of the road and parks, practically crushing me against the passenger seat as he kisses me.

"You're going to have to behave," he tells me. "Until we get to where we're going."

"And where is that?" I ask against his lips.

"Our date," he reminds me. "We're playing hooky today. We're got a theory to test out. Now, you sit over there and be good. I'll drive."

He looks at me, his eyebrow raised. I nod.

"Fine," I answer. "If you can't multi-task, then I'll behave." Alex practically growls as he pulls back into the road and I have to laugh.

He drives us straight to the Stratosphere Hotel. It's a staple in the Las Vegas landscape and to be honest, since I'm a local, I've never actually stayed in the hotel.

"Why are we here?" I ask as he parks the car.

"We have a date," he growls.

He guides my elbow as we check in. I press myself discreetly against him as he signs the registration form and he gives me a sidelong gaze. I step away and return his gaze innocently. When he returns his attention to the form, I press myself against him again. He sighs.

But it isn't long before we're in the elevator and he turns to me.

"We're alone," he points out. And that's all it takes.

I'm in his arms immediately, inhaling his sexy-as-hell scent and wrapping my tongue around his. It's funny how when you fantasize about someone, typically you don't find out how they would actually be in person. I am pleased to report that Alex is ten million times better than my fantasies.

He pins me to the gold mirrored wall, his hand sliding up between my legs.

"You're wet for me," he whispers in my ear. "I can tell through your panties. Today of all days, why did you wear panties?"

I laugh. "I told you, I usually do."

"New rule," he says with a growl. "No panties."

I laugh as I grab him through his slacks. He is so hard that there is a perfect indention of his penis through his pants. I shove it against me, grinding it into me. He groans again which totally turns me on.

"New rule," I tell him. "No pants. Ever."

It's his turn to chuckle. "That might make meetings at work awkward. Although, you somehow manage it."

I glare at him as my fingers tighten around him through his pants. "One time. One freaking time and I'm never going to hear the end of it, am I?"

He's already shaking his head and laughing. "Alli, I'm sorry, but that particular incident was too good to ever let you forget it."

I'm rolling my eyes as the elevator glides to a stop and the doors open, letting two other people on. The younger couple looks at us and we separate. I know my cheeks are flushed.

Alex flashes me a you're-going-to-get-it look. I flush again.

The elevator finally stops on our floor and we hurry out and down the hall. Alex slides the key in the lock and we tumble through the door. I drop my purse and turn to him and he shoves me against the wall, lifting my ass in his hands as he pushes his tongue into my mouth.

This moment is hot and primal and I totally give in to it.

My delicate silk shirt doesn't last long. It's ripped off within a minute and I watch the torn fabric bits fall to the floor. My stockings follow and then I'm lifted again, my legs wrapped around Alex's strong hips. One quick rustle of foil and then he's sliding into me with my skirt shoved up around my waist.

I gasp, pulling him closer, pulling his head into my breasts. He sucks there; licking, lapping, nipping. I moan and he rams into me harder. The wall grates against my back, but I don't even notice it. All I can focus on is Alex's ragged breathing, his beautiful body, his intoxicating smell and this erotic moment.

He grabs me and carries me to the bed with my legs wrapped around his waist. He lays me down quickly with his hand beneath my head, kissing me so thoroughly that I think I will go insane unless he's inside of me again.

"Please," I tell him, pulling at him.

"Please what?" he asks impishly, purposely resisting my fingers.

"Please fuck me," I tell him, remembering Shade's words. *Men like naughty words.*

Alex smiles wickedly. "Fuck you how?" he asks softly as he slides into me.

"Fuck me hard," I tell him. "I've been waiting for this forever."

He inhales and grabs me, sliding into me roughly. And he does fuck me hard. After a while, he flips me over and enters me from behind, pulling my head back by my hair with just the right amount of pressure.

Oh, my lord.

This is erotic and primal and almost desperate, because the sexual tension has built up for so long. And now it is exploding.

After I shout his name and collapse onto the bed, Alex throws his head back and comes with a shudder. And then he drops into a heap next to me. He is damp and so am I. He reaches over and brushes my hair out of my eye.

"That was amazing," he tells me. "You're a wildcat."

I smile. "I think the proper term is cougar."

He chuckles and I nestle into his side. "I thought cougars dated younger men?"

A pang shoots through me, but I set it aside. That's a part of my life that is private. I never have to reveal it. So, I smile instead.

"Oh, I like to think that a cougar is simply a mature woman who knows what she wants- both in the bedroom and out."

"Oh, you certainly are that," Alex agrees.

We lay entwined on the plush bed for the next half hour, relaxing and chatting softly. Finally, I look up at him.

"I think we're sexually compatible."

He laughs. "Um, yes. I think that is safe to say. Not that I ever had any doubts."

He bends his head and kisses me, gently this time. The sense of desperation is gone now and so this time, we allow ourselves the luxury of being slow and relaxed.

He slides his hands everywhere and tells me that I'm beautiful. I mimic his movements and tell him the same.

"Men aren't beautiful," he says with a smile as he kisses my neck.

"You are," I argue as I cover his lips with my own.

And then he makes love to me. And it does feel like making love. With Shade, it was never that. It was sex… it was fucking… it was fucking amazing. But it wasn't making love.

With Alex….there is something here between us. Something amazing. And something tender and sweet and sexy and fucking hot. And it does feel like making love. And we make love three more times before we realize that it is 3:00 pm.

"Look at the time!" I exclaim as I finally glance at the clock. "Sophie will be getting home from school in an hour or so."

"Can you call and tell her that you'll be late?" Alex asks as he sits on the side of the bed. "We have a shower to take and then I think I could use some food for sustenance."

I glance at him. "Sustenance?"

Alex laughs. "I'm not as young as I used to be. I require food and drink after having sex four times. We were supposed to have brunch, you know, until you distracted me with your feminine wiles."

I stare at him. "Um, you impaled my leg with your penis in my office. You're hardly innocent in this."

He laughs again.

I shake my head and let him pull me to the big stone shower. Where, even though he hasn't had any sustenance yet, we have sex for a fifth time.

As the steam covers us up and with my face pressed against the foggy shower glass, Alex fills me up yet again. I've never felt so fulfilled.

And being with him seems so unbelievably right.

"We fit, Alli Cat," he whispers in my ear and I freeze, turning into him.

"Alli Cat?" I ask tremulously. Surely Colby hadn't said anything to him. *Surely.* That would be sick on so many levels. But Alex's face is open and honest and unfazed as he answers.

"You're my wild little Alli Cat, "he replies. And I can tell that he just made the name up. He has no idea that his son has used it before him. "And we do fit perfectly together."

"We do," I admit with a sigh. "What are we going to do about that?"

"We'll figure it out," he says with a shrug. "We're two intelligent adults."

When we get out of the shower, I find a text from Sophie. She's going to Hayley's to do homework and won't be home until later.

I turn to Alex. "I'm free for dinner. But there is a small problem... you ripped my shirt off. I can't go naked."

Alex grins. "I guess we're even now. You ruined a pair of my pants and I ruined one of your shirts. The score is tied, milady."

I laugh and he ducks out to buy me a shirt in the gift shop.

And that is how Alex and I end up in the World Restaurant in the top of the Stratosphere having dinner while I wear an oversized souvenir t-shirt, a dress skirt and kick-ass heels. And of course, we are eating steak.

"You know, too much steak will clog your arteries," I tell Alex with a grin. He shrugs again, unconcerned.

"I've earned it today, I think," he says mischievously. And I can't argue with that. He *has* earned it today.

"This is a gorgeous view," I say as I gaze at the Vegas horizon, with its skyscrapers and desert and dying sunshine.

"Not as gorgeous as mine," Alex says as he stares at me. His words would be cheesy if it weren't for the intense expression in his blue eyes. I inhale. Sharply.

"You know we're good together," he says as he sips his drink.

I don't even bother to lie.

"Yes," I answer simply.

"And your only issue is that we work together, correct?" Alex swallows his drink and motions for the waiter to bring him another.

I nod.

"Well, that's an easy fix then," he says, leveling his gaze at me. "You're fired."

Chapter Twenty-One

(Or: What the Eff?)

"What?" I squeak, staring at him in astonishment and horror. "No. I don't want that."

Alex looks at me in bemusement.

"I don't mean that you're actually fired right this minute. But I have a solution, if you'd like to hear it."

I try to soothe my pounding heart, to get a grip on myself.

"Yes, I'd like to hear it, as long as it doesn't involve me getting fired. I've worked hard to get where I'm at, Alex."

"I know you have," he nods. "And I'm not the only one who has noticed. Remember when I told you that headhunters have asked about you? One of them is my friend, Tom. The friend who found this job for me. He's asked about you. Apparently, there is a job at a nearby winery that would be perfect for you."

"A winery in Las Vegas?" I ask doubtfully. Alex smiles.

"Well, it's a little over an hour away, across the California border. But it's an easy commute."

"And why would I switch jobs?" I ask a little heatedly. "I like what I'm doing now."

"Well," Alex says slowly. "It's a vice president position. And it's at a winery. You love wine. And if you take a better job, then you're no longer working for me. Which means that our little problem is solved."

I stare at him silently, trying to wrap my mind around his words.

"I do love wine," I say absently.

"Yes, you do," Alex agrees with a smile.

"And I would like a vice president position," I say uncertainly.

"Yes, you would," Alex agrees again. "And you deserve a vice president position. And unfortunately, your only path to getting that position at Zellers is through me—to take my job. And I'm not going anywhere anytime soon. So…"

"So this is a perfect proposition for me," I sum up, looking at him.

"It would seem that way," he says, sipping at his drink again. "But take your time and think about it. I've got Tom's card. You can give him a call to discuss it, if you would like."

I feel a little stunned. Everything seems to be happening so fast.

But I have to admit. Completely starting over, like Alex did, seems a little fascinating.

"You set this up, didn't you?" I ask. "You contacted your friend, not the other way around."

I can see on his face that I am right.

He shrugs. "I just put some feelers out there. You and I have had chemistry from the beginning. Once I was contacted by someone else about you, it gave me the idea to check. The position really is a perfect fit for you, Alli. You would be heading up the marketing department. It's exactly what you do and do well. Plus, did I mention… you would be marketing wine."

I sigh because he's piqued my curiosity. It does sound perfect for me.

"I love wine," I sigh. "Okay. I'll call your friend."

"Excellent," Alex says with a smile, holding his glass up. "Here's to new beginnings."

There are a lot of promises in his smile and I know that he isn't just talking about new beginnings with my career. I gulp and clink glasses.

"To new beginnings," I say awkwardly.

Alex gazes at me.

"What's wrong?"

I shake my head. "You're going to think I'm silly."

"Probably not," he answers. "Just tell me."

"I have a problem now…with commitment. After I invested fifteen years of my life with Rick and he cheated on me, I find it a little disconcerting to just trust you with so many areas of my life. I guess I have trust issues."

Alex nods slowly. And he is so, so handsome. I try to ignore that fact.

"I understand," he tells me. "But I want you to know…I'm a trustworthy person. And I don't expect you to trust me immediately. I expect to earn your trust. And I will, I promise."

His tone is soothing and husky and it warms me. I smile. He already knows exactly how to talk me off of the ledge. *He's what I need.*

We finish our dinner and check out of the hotel. He drops me back off at my car and kisses me soundly.

"I'll call you later," he tells me. I nod.

I go home, pour a glass of wine and do what any rational woman would do.

I get in the hot tub and call Sara.

She arrives thirty minutes later and climbs in with me. This time, we wear our swimsuits since Sophie is indoors.

"I don't see what the big question is," Sara announces after I've finished explaining. "He's arranged for a chance for you to get a better job so that you can date him. And he's eligible, handsome, sexy and perfect. At least, he seems to be. I can't say for certain, since I haven't personally met him."

She pauses here, a long pregnant pause with her eyebrow raised.

"What?" I ask. "You can meet him. Someday. In probably forty years or so. I don't want you to scare him to death."

"I'm not a scary person," she sniffs. "Seriously. It's within my rights to meet him, Alli. It's the only way that I can make an accurate judgment call on this."

"I don't need your accurate judgment call," I tell her. "I think I've got this."

"Then why did you call me, genius?" she asks. "You wanted my opinion, that's why."

"Maybe," I acknowledge. "But I wanted it without you intimidating Alex for it."

I take a long drink of my wine and lay my head back. Sara lays hers back too.

"Just trust me, sweetie. I won't embarrass you. I simply have a handful of questions for the man. Besides, the man's a big important VP hot-shot. I can't intimidate him, I'm sure. Seriously. How bad could it possibly be?"

No one should ever ask a question like that.

I know that. I knew it when she said it and I knew it four days later when I wanted to kill her. Again.

****

"How do I know that you can keep your dick in your pants?" Sara asks conversationally over a dinner of take-out Chinese and expensive wine on my patio.

She, of course, is speaking to Alex. After pestering me all week, I finally agreed to let her have dinner with us tonight. And it was a mistake of the biggest possible kind. But Alex is taking it in stride and is even seemingly amused.

I'm even further impressed with him, if that is even possible.

Alex smiles at Sara. "Well, my dick is forty years old. It doesn't have the energy to go venturing out of my pants into strange waters."

She studies him. "Well, that would be a good answer, but Rick was almost the same age and his dick found the energy."

Alex sighs good-naturedly. "I'm not Rick the Dick, though," he points out.

I nod. That is a very valid point. This interrogation has gone on for over an hour now. And I have to say that he's handling Sara very well.

"True," Sara says, gazing at him. "And that's probably the best answer you can give me."

Alex shoots me a glance behind Sara's skinny back.

She means well, I mouth to him. He nods.

"I'll get us another bottle of wine, ladies," he says, standing up. As he walks into the house, Sara calls to him.

"You've got a really nice ass! That's one point in your favor."

Alex turns and grins before heading into the house.

"Seriously, Sara," I hiss. "Oh my god. You're embarrassing."

"But I feel much better now," she tells me. "Okay. I've decided. You have my permission. You can date him. The sex is good, he's gorgeous, he's sexy…what's not to like?"

She takes a nonchalant bite of her eggroll, as if it is really her decision to make. I sigh.

"You forgot patient," I tell her. "He's very patient."

She levels a gaze at me. "True, he's patient."

"And I don't need your permission, "I remind her. "But thank you, nonetheless."

Alex returns and pours us each a glass of wine. I fight the urge to lean into him and kiss him. He's sexy as hell, damn it. And he smells good, too. But then Sara distracts me with a question.

"This is all a little sudden. What does Sophie think?"

I am silent as I stare at Alex.

"You haven't told Sophie yet?" Sara is incredulous. "How have you been seeing each other all week without her noticing?"

"Okay, first of all. This isn't sudden. We're moving a little quickly, but that's only because we're mature adults who are sure about what we want," I tell her. "There's no reason to wait. And second, we haven't told Sophie because it isn't time yet."

Sara stares at me, unconvinced. "And when will be the time?"

"I don't know," I admit quietly. "Soon."

"And what about the new job?" Sara asks. "What have you decided?"

I gaze at Alex over the table. He gives me an encouraging look.

"I'm going to meet with the winery owners next week," I tell her. "And if it is actually as good of an opportunity as it sounds like, I think I'll probably take it."

Sara sits back in her seat, staring first to me, then to Alex.

"Well, it looks like everything is pretty sewn up here," she says. "My work here is done."

Alex raises a sexy eyebrow. "*Your* work?"

"Yep," Sara answers before I can kick her. "It's because of me that Alli got out there in the first place. She'd never have been ready to date you if I hadn't stepped in."

"Oh?" Alex asks, his eyes meeting mine.

"Yes," I interject quickly. "Sara talked me into going on a date with Brian from Accounting. Just for practice," I tell him. He's understandably surprised.

"Brian from Accounting?" he repeats skeptically. I nod.

"Yep and it was about as fun as you'd imagine."

Alex laughs, slow and easy, and changes the subject.

We finish off the new bottle of wine before Sara takes her leave, making sure she slaps Alex on the ass on her way out. He shakes his head as we walk indoors.

"Your friend is a character," he tells me.

"Everyone says that," I laugh. "Character, firecracker, saucy wench…take your pick."

"But I like her," he replies. "She tells it like it is and I have to respect that."

He sits down on the sofa and pulls me down with him. He kisses the side of my neck and then pulls away, looking at me.

"So, I may or may not be mistaken, but I think you were ready to have a panic attack when Sara started talking about getting you ready for me. Am I right?"

I am frozen now. I have no idea what to say. I certainly can't tell him the truth.

Why, yes, Alex. Sara talked me into having sex with a gigolo who turned out to be your son. No. That wouldn't be good. I obviously can't say that. I'm like a deer caught in the headlights. My mouth opens, then closes. I don't know what to say.

Alex studies me. "Don't feel self-conscious about anyone you might have dated before me," he tells me. "It's not my business. You were just divorced. Of course you needed to go out and get crazy. That's expected. And I'm sure you were safe about it. Honestly, I'm glad Sara talked you into it. Because now you're ready for me."

I am silent and astounded by his most perfect of answers.

I can continue on with him without feeling guilty about Colby because Alex has just given me a pass. It's expected, he says. *Expected.* I hardly doubt that having sex with his son is what he meant but that's a detail, right?

I nod slowly. "I might have gotten a little carried away," I say carefully. "But that's over now. I like being with you. You and I are perfect."

And now he laughs. "We won't always be perfect," he tells me, pulling me closer into his lap. "But we're perfect for each other. Of that, I have no doubt. When do you want to tell our kids?"

Our kids.

Colby.

I want to freaking die right now.

If Alex and I ever get married, Colby will be my step-son. The guy who taught me how to bring a guy to his knees in five minutes flat will be my step-son.

I may need therapy.

But then again, to be fair, Colby has been true to his word. This entire last week at work, he has pretended like we are only just now getting to know each other, like the only other way we know each other is because he's Sophie's swim coach. And just like he said, it's starting to seem less weird. Like I am truly just his boss and he is truly just my intern.

The son of the guy I'm dating.

But I'm working through that. And the more time that goes by, the more normal it seems. I can totally do this. And Colby does seem genuinely happy for his dad.

"I don't know," I tell him. "I think Sophie will be fine. I mean, she hates her father's fiancée, but Vanessa is barely older than Soph and she is an utter bitch. So, there's a difference."

"You think I'll be fine about what?"

Sophie's voice floats through the living room and my head snaps up. My eyes meet hers. And I remember that I am sitting on Alex's lap.

"Um."

I don't even know what to say. I'm that shocked. I scramble off of Alex's lap and practically break my neck to get across the room to her.

"Well, we were talking about you and what you would say...if...Alex and I started dating."

My tone is more like a question than a statement.

Sophie stares at me.

"But you're already dating," she answers matter-of-factly. "If you wanted my permission, don't you think you should have asked ahead of time?"

I'm appalled now as I stare at her, aghast.

"How did you know?" I whisper. Alex is behind me now, one hand on the small of my back. He starts to say something, but Sophie interrupts with a smile.

"Well, you were just sitting on his lap, mom." I blush and she laughs. "I'm kidding, Mom. Yes, I knew...because I'm not stupid. You were making random excuses to go to his house for work and he kept 'forgetting' files here so he'd have to come back. You guys were soooo obvious. But it's okay- I'm fine with it. You guys are cute."

And she sounds like she's talking to her child instead of her parent.

I'm staring at her blankly.

She smiles again and she looks angelic.

"Seriously, mom. It's fine. I'm happy for you. And I'm happy that Alex isn't a dick like my dad. Or Vanessa."

And she gives me a little hug and is trotting off down the hall before I can gather my wits.

"Don't call your father a dick!" I shout to her. And then I turn to Alex.

"Well, one child down," I say limply.

"One child to go," he says. "But Colby will be fine. I'm pretty sure of that."

I'm already sure of that, but I don't say anything. Instead, I just smile and walk to the kitchen, pouring us each another glass of wine.

God, I love wine.

****

Alex tells Colby the following week.

Colby took it just fine, like I knew he would. In fact, he came into my office and congratulated me shortly afterward.

"I seriously want you to be happy, Alli," he says, leaning forward in his seat and giving me his boyish grin. "And my dad too. You really are perfect for each other."

"I think so, too," I tell him. "Thank you."

"And things aren't going to be weird between us," he says. "I can tell right now. You're one chill chick. You just take things as they come. I like that. It's just what my dad needs."

I smile. I don't feel like a 'chill chick' whatever that is, but I don't point that out or even ask for a definition.

"And also, you'll be happy to know...I'm quitting Utopia. I sort of like being here at Zeller's and I can't be a gigolo my whole life. I need to do something a little more respectable. So, I'm going to graduate school, after all. I think it's what I need to do."

I'm shocked now as I stare at him.

"You were a really good gigolo," I tell him. "But you'll be a great businessman, too."

He smiles his charming grin. "Thank you. And of course, I still intend to coach Sophie, until she is at a level where she needs a professional coach."

"Of course," I answer. "I appreciate it."

He leans over and kisses my cheek and it doesn't feel sexual at all.

I really think I can do this. I can carry this off.

And later in the week, after my interview with the owners of the winery, I decide to take the job. On the condition that I can bring my own assistant, of course. Taylor is fiery and annoying at times, but she takes good care of me. I wouldn't leave her behind.

This is a notion that baffles me though after listening to her endless complaints about packing up my office stuff and the fact that her new commute will be longer than it is right now.

I stare at her.

"Taylor, we'll be working in a winery. *A winery.* Enough said." She glares at me and stalks out, but not before I see her smile. She's going to love it. As will I.

I'm packing up a last box when Alex comes in, wrapping his arms around me from behind.

I sigh a happy sigh.

I had no idea that I would be this happy in such a short amount of time. BB practically sings to me every day—that's how satisfied and happy she is. You know what they say...a happy vagina is a happy woman. Well, they might not say that, but they should.

"What do you think?" Alex asks as he brushes a kiss along the crook of my neck, right where I like it. "Are you sad to leave?"

I look around at the plush corner office that I worked so hard to get. And I know that I'm not sad, because I'm winning on so many different levels. I'm going to a better office. Win. And it's surrounded by grapevines. Double Win. I'm dating a fabulous and sexy guy who is successful and confident. Triple Win.

Everything seems to be clicking into place, like it was meant to happen this way.

I read somewhere that every broken road in life leads to where you were meant to go in the first place. Or something like that. And it really is true. I thought I was meant to be with Rick the Dick and live until we were old and gray in a corner room of the retirement home. But he had other plans...and so did Life.

Life threw grapes at me but I turned them into wine.

God, I love wine.

I turn to Alex. "No, I'm not sad. I'm not sad at all."

Then he kisses me until my knees grow weak.

And I know beyond any shadow of any doubt that I'm doing the right thing…regarding every aspect of my life. My knees were meant to be made weak by this man.

"Kiss me again," I tell him.

So he does.

Epilogue

"You can stack that over there," I tell a mover. The movers all appear to be burly and rough around the edges, but I gave them doughnuts for breakfast, so they like me. This one grunts and moves the box.

"Hey sweetie," Alex calls from our bedroom. "How do you want me to label this box?"

I walk back and find that he has packed up my bedside stand and all of the glorious toys that it contained. Over the course of the past year, I added a few companions for Geronimo. And Alex and I use them regularly…together. Hey, don't judge. It's freaking hot.

"Um, how about Sex Toys?" I suggest. He rolls his eyes and writes ALLI'S NIGHTSTAND- –PRIVATE.

"As if no one will know what that means," I giggle.

"Are you absolutely sure that you want to move?" Alex asks for the twenty-fifth time. I glance at him.

"I think that after having a gorgeous new house built on the edge of a vineyard, we'd probably better move, don't you think?" I ask wryly.

Alex stares at me. "I just know that Sophie grew up here. You have a lot of memories here. I don't want you to leave unless you are sure you want to."

I smile. "You are the sexiest, most handsome man on the planet. It was my idea to move. I want to start our marriage in our own house. Not *my* house."

He grins. "Mrs. Harris. I'm really loving the sound of that. Although, just know that you will never be allowed to take tennis lessons." I smile, remembering that his bitch of an ex-wife cheated on him with a tennis instructor.

"Don't worry," I say. "I hate tennis."

"I knew I loved you for a reason," he jokes as he seals up my toys.

"You love me for a *lot* of reasons," I answer.

He nods. "I won't argue there, Alli Cat."

The first time Colby overheard Alex calling me Alli Cat, I think he almost choked on his tongue. But he recovered quickly and things have been very normal on that front.

Colby is one year into his MBA program and he's doing very well at Zellers. My replacement quickly promoted him from an intern to an entry level manager because of Colby's initiative and drive. I know from personal experience that the boy's got initiative. And drive.

Sophie is kicking ass at swimming and taking names. She's well on her way to winning at State levels and then she can swim in college. And who knows how far she'll go after that?

Rick the Dick is alone. Vanessa broke up with him shortly after Alex and I got together. I seldom have to see him, but when I do, we manage to be civil. He's a dick, but he's not *my* dick anymore. He can cause someone else grief. Someday, that is, when he convinces someone else to date him.

And Sara… my devil of a best friend is dating Tom, Alex's recruiter friend who got me the job at the winery. She called him up to check on the job market and they somehow wound up dating. Sara's good at flipping a situation like that. She's going to be my maid-of-honor, of course, and she's already got all kinds of top-secret things planned for my bachelorette party. I'm terrified already.

Oh, and the winery. Alex ended up buying into the winery, so we're part owners now. He gave it to me as an engagement present. He proposed on a cliff in Hawaii when we were there this past summer. It was romantic and sweet and perfect. Just like Alex. The ring I'm wearing on my finger is enormous. So huge and sparkling that it made Sara howl with envy, which of course is important.

Last but not least, my girl BB is as satisfied as a cat with a belly full of milk. Or make that a *cougar* with a full belly. She gets waxed regularly now, every three months or so. And that Waxer Girl was totally right. It doesn't hurt nearly as much after the first or second time. BB is bald and proud of it. She's a sassy wench.

"Alli?"

I can tell by Alex's tone that it's not the first time he's said my name.

I turn to him, staring at the way the morning sunlight falls against his handsome face. I stroke a hand where the light hits him.

"Yes?" I ask sweetly.

"I was just going to ask where you wanted to get brunch. But never mind. I have a better idea in mind."

He strides across the room and locks the bedroom door and then pushes me onto the bed with the wicked grin that I so, so love.

The movers can wait.

Acknowledgements

Holy cow. I have a lot of people to thank for this book.

M. Leighton. My partner in crime and BFF. Thank you for everything. Thank you for brainstorming with me and for pushing me to finish writing this book. I don't know what I'd do without you. I can't wait until we move to the Keys and have adjoining secret passages to each other's wine cellars.

My husband. Thank you again for putting up with me and keeping me around. Thank you, too, for giving me the "Drop a man to his knees in five minutes" scene. I can't help but wonder if that was self-serving in any way, shape or form... but oh, well. I love you anyway and I'll keep you. Hehe.

To my Cougars! Rawrrrr! Thank you, ladies, for your early input on Alli's story...for your enthusiasm and for just being downright awesome.

Tracy Mims
Megan Ridgeway
Marcia Woodell
Courtney DeLollis
Maria Vargas
Autumn Hull

Michelle Files
Drita Kinic
Danielle Morales
Christina Pryor

Tammy Luke—thank you for being my patient and amazing cover artist.

And thank YOU, my awesome and amazing readers. Without you, I wouldn't have the best job in the world. I love what I do and I am thankful for you every single day of my life.

About the Author

Courtney Cole is a novelist who lives near Lake Michigan with her domestic zoo (AKA family), her pet iPad and her favorite cashmere socks. To learn more about her, visit www.courtneycolewrites.com

Other books by Courtney Cole:

The Paradise Diaries (YA, Contemporary)
Dante's Girl
Mia's Heart (Coming Soon)

The Bloodstone Saga (YA/NA, Paranormal Romance)
Every Last Kiss
Fated
With My Last Breath
My Tattered Bonds
House of Thebes

The Moonstone Saga (YA/NA, Paranormal Romance)
Soul Kissed
Soul Bound
Princess of the Moon (Coming Soon)

The Minaldi Legacy (Dark Romance/Contemporary)
Of Blood and Bone